FOR AS LONG AS SHE CAN REMEMBER, SEG HAS LIVED IN THE ORPHANAGE.

She was brought there by her spiteful mentor, Plumbess Roc, to
learn the art and danger of Plumbing—to become a Plumbess.
But when Seg struggles, when she finds nightmares
in Plumbing's dark recesses,
she always turns to another Plumbess—
the warm, caring Plumbess Zag—for solace.

UNTIL ZAG DIES.

Seg blames Eck for Zag's death—Eck who was raised by snakes,
Eck who left a scar on Seg's neck when they were children.
When Seg finally leaves the Orphanage to
find a Pipe Lord and do her work,
she's weighed down by loss, hatred, and
the heavy Lead around her neck, which reopens her old scar.
But she takes her plunger in hand and follows the pipes,
even though they lead back to her nightmares—and back to Eck.

PLUMBESS SEG

a novel by

JUDE FAWLEY

S T I C K S   R I V E R

STICKS RIVER

This book is a work of fiction. Names, characters, places, and incidents
either are products of the author's imagination or are used fictitiously.
Any resemblance to actual events or locales or persons,
living or dead, is entirely coincidental.

PLUMBESS SEG

DESIGNED BY KARL PFEIFFER

Cover art by Preston Stone © 2019

All graphic design work copyright © 2019 Karl Pfeiffer
Sticks River is the design imprint of Karl Pfeiffer Photography

Text set in Times New Roman and the Garamond family.

Produced in the United States of America

ISBN-13: 978-1720945109
ISBN-10: 1720945101

Fiction

FIRST EDITION

For the Dry Princess

PLUMBESS
SEG

BEGINNING AGAIN

AFTER DECADES, AFTER days of raining, it finally stopped. Perhaps that wasn't the clearest way to express it. But it *had* rained enough that liters or centimeters weren't the proper unit of measurement—it was at least a decade of rain.

Firmly in the realm of time, it had shortened lives, turned days into nights, and confined Seg to her bed for longer than she could comprehend, until the days felt like years and the nights even longer.

After such a humiliating defeat, the sun had yet to show itself, but the clouds looked like the kind that would eventually go away. Seg wasn't an expert on clouds, though. She watched them through her bedroom window.

Entrenched in her sheets like the patron saint of consumption, she stirred.

Ten days before, ten days in the normal sense of time, a village called Flotsam had been washed away in the rain's torrent. Seg didn't care about the village, but Zag—the only person who had meant anything at all to her—had been in Flotsam, trying to save it from the flood like only a Plumbess could. No one had seen her since.

Except for Seg, in her dreams. Just the night before, Seg had descended one of those dark abysses, the kind that collected all the world's rains in its hidden depths. If Zag truly had been washed away, that was where she would be. Without a single light to guide her, she found all the rain, and Zag at its center. The Plumbess stood imperiously, a statue of a shade, her plunger held out before her, lethal and serene. It was a monument to power. But it wasn't what Seg was looking for. She didn't need a monument, she needed a person. *The* person. Seg spoke, she pled that she might hear the Plumbess's voice, but she knew the futility of the effort. The night before had been the same—she'd found Zag in the ocean, in the form of an island holding a slender peninsula that defied all waves. The same silence, a larger body of water than Seg could ever hope to conquer.

Getting out of her bed was harder than descending the rain's abyss, but she did it. She took a few faltering steps to her wardrobe and struggled to open it. Inside, there weren't any clothes fit for a healthy person. She pulled on some boots heavy enough for a calamitous amount of mud—she wanted something with a thick sole. She threw a raincoat over her shoulders even though it wasn't raining anymore. For the most part it covered her nightdress, the one she'd been wearing for a decade now. And, finally, an umbrella, which she held on to the same way a Plumbess would hold a plunger.

She opened her door and exited to the hallway beyond. That hallway led to another, and another, not a person to be seen, just closed doors and silent pipes wending their way deeper. Slowly she unwound her way out of their maze and into the outside world. She stood near the Top of the Incline, the top third of the massive structure that dominated the center of the Orphanage. Although the Orphanage was at the bottom of a valley, it would easily weather any storm. The smell of rain, though, was overwhelming. She took a deep breath.

To assist with the spiraling descent down the Incline was a railing of the finest quality. Where other railings would be hollow, this one was filled with a slow liquid, calm and soothing. Holding on to it helped Seg immensely. She let it guide her downward.

The people who saw her didn't bother hiding their stares. A few even made the holy sign, a touch of the lip followed by a touch of the navel. She inverted the gesture at an orphan, barely pubescent: she touched her navel then her lips, counter to all nature. The orphan reddened and turned away, back to her menial task—tracing pipes around the limits of her permitted range.

Others were more tactful, but Seg treated them the same.

"I'm sorry, Seg, but it is good to see you again."

"It's good to be seen, you're sorry," she replied, inverting the gesture no matter what sense it gave.

Around the Middle of the Incline, she was confronted again.

"Ms. Seg? Plumbess Roc wanted to be informed if you ever left your room again. Would you like me to tell her?"

"I'll tell her myself," Seg replied.

She slowly regained confidence. She let her nose rise preternaturally high, and her back became straighter than a wall joist, more rigid, with the result that she couldn't even see most of the things around her.

Thus it was an invisible orphan who spoke the words that nearly broke her composure all over again.

"Ms. Seg, it's you! Have you seen Ms. Eck? She was your friend, right?"

Hatred welled up in her like a river in a broken dam. "If you don't know the meaning of words, orphan, you shouldn't use them. Eck never was and never will be my friend."

Seg never looked at the child, but she heard it scamper off.

Eck, her friend. Seg could've saved Zag, could've saved herself, if it hadn't been for Eck. The valve had been in her hands, and a firm resolve in her heart, but that scaly subhuman had stopped her—had *stopped* her, when she was the only person who could have made a difference. Before she had devoted herself to her despondence, Seg had driven Eck out of the Orphanage. And although she thought she'd made a scene, apparently the nature of the event, of Eck's betrayal, hadn't made its way through the Orphanage yet. She would tell them all.

At the Bottom of the Incline, hundreds of people scurried about, which was nearly the entire population of the Orphanage. Plumbess Roc stood in the center of the commotion, apparently directing it. Several people stood attentively at the Plumbess's side as she handled them individually.

Seg approached them.

The old Plumbess was a shriveled thing, her grey hair tied up in knots around her head. The skin of her face was tight, readily emphasizing her expressions of disapproval. Although she carried her plunger around as any Plumbess would, and currently used it to indicate something to the people around her, it didn't exude the strength that it had with Plumbess Zag.

She was yelling at a nearby man. "Move it over there, I said. And stop asking so many questions!"

The man nodded and hurried off.

When Seg noticed that Roc intended to begin yelling at the next man, another of the Orphanage's servants, she cleared her throat.

"Yes?" the Plumbess started angrily, but broke off when she noticed that it was Seg. "Oh, it's you. Finally."

"Finally?" Seg asked, with an air of confrontation. Seg was a full foot taller, and looked decidedly down at the Plumbess. "Has my sorrow inconvenienced you in some way?"

"It's inconvenienced us all," Roc replied. "I know Plumbess Zag was important to you, but she was just as important to me."

Seg nearly snorted in derision, but refrained.

Roc noticed anyway. "I will not, I repeat, I will not be condescended to by a naïve little thing like you, do you hear me? She was just as important to me. But a true Plumbess can't give herself away to her emotions, especially not when the need is dire."

Roc gestured with her plunger to what the crowd was working on: disassembling a series of impromptu ditches made to redirect the storm. "We have a duty to uphold. You should've been here helping. The gods know we could've used you. So yes, *finally*."

"Only a Plumbess could've helped," Seg said, a bitter mimicry leaching into her voice.

"And in spite of everything, I still intend to make you one. Are you ready?"

"When?"

"When, girl? Now! It should've been a week ago, when it was scheduled, but even I can let go of a schedule if the winds demand it. That is, if you truly are ready. Are you ready?"

A valid question, Seg thought—she wasn't sure herself. So, she appraised herself the way she would've appraised a newly welded joint. She took both ends in her hand—the pipe of her life before losing Zag, and the pipe of her life after—and she twisted. Any hint of hesitation in the weld, the slightest slip, and she would feel it. And although the one pipe was short and jagged, dangerous to the touch, the weld itself was of passable workmanship.

"Yes, I am."

"Then get your things, girl, and meet me by the gate."

Seg didn't need to be told twice. She turned around and retraced her steps back up the Incline. Her thoughts, while she walked, gravitated back to Eck.

Although what she'd said to Roc was true, and she was ready to continue her life, one thing was for certain: her hatred of Eck was insurmountable, a septic tank overloaded beyond repair.

How could the Plumbesses have ever paired them as if they were equals? If Eck was within a five-kilometer radius, Seg would find her and drown her in the aqueducts. She imagined stabbing Eck, tearing her limb from limb, welding her shut, tying a cinch around her neck and tightening it degree by degree until her face turned red, then purple, then . . .

Ways to kill Eck provided Seg with enough ammunition of

thought to bring her all the way back to her room, where the weight of her sadness quieted her again.

She took off her thick-soled boots, made for the mud but spotless because she'd never left the path of the Incline. She took off her raincoat, dry because it would probably be another year before the sky gathered enough moisture again to even think about raining. And she removed her nightgown, which she should've done at least a week before. Divested of such clothes, she opened up her wardrobe again.

There was only one set of clothes suitable for what she was to become. Far to the right—past the clothes she'd worn threadbare from working on her hands and knees in narrow, dark places—hung an immaculate white apron and a black linen shirt. She put these on, as well as a black pair of pants, practical things that covered her legs entirely. Next came a black pair of rubber boots, and even a black pair of rubber gloves for the occasion. And finally, her plunger. She'd had it for years, but was only allowed to carry it for special occasions.

Next to the wardrobe was a full-length mirror. Staring back at her, eyes sunken but vividly alive, was a Plumbess. Younger than any Plumbess she'd ever seen, her skin paler and her hair blacker, but a Plumbess nonetheless. To test the authenticity of the image, she brought her plunger into it—over her shoulder, like a Plumbess at the ready. She struck the ground with it violently, forming suction against the wood. It looked convincing, that image. That was more than she could ask for.

Since she wouldn't be coming back, at least not for a long time, she packed what little possessions she had into a white sack that she slung over her shoulder. Then, because it felt like something a person should do when leaving the only home they'd ever had, she took a farewell glance at her room.

For all the time she'd spent there, she hadn't left much of a mark. A conspicuous indentation in the mattress. Some muddy footprints in the doorway, ten days dry, which would be gone the next time the room was scrubbed clean. The half-spent candle in the windowsill, for all she'd personally burned it, was no doubt indistinguishable from others in that very same hallway.

"Goodbye," she said anyway.

This time, going down the Incline, she was strong enough, body and spirit, to forgo the railing. She struck it once with her plunger, sending vibrations she could feel down its whole length, and then she ignored it like she'd never once depended on its solace.

This time, she gave a resolute nod to every downtrodden orphan, to every uptight Plumbess who crossed her path. It was apparent that they already knew what was going on—the people she passed soon formed into a retinue of sorts, conversing as they followed her down to the gate of the Orphanage.

Roc already stood there, an impatient look on her face. It reminded Seg of a time ten years before, when, instead of a plunger over her shoulder, Seg had the full spectrum of shovels. For an instant, she nearly conceded to an impulse to hasten her steps. But she repressed the impulse just as she repressed the memory. Those were things best forgotten.

The old Plumbess said, when Seg joined her, "I'll ask you one last time if you're ready. There won't be any turning back after this."

As if she hadn't been waiting ten years to get rid of Seg.

Roc had once said, in a garden not far removed, that she'd wasted her life mentoring her.

"I'm aware of that," Seg replied. "And I already said I was."

"Very well," Roc said, and then projected her voice with a volume unbecoming of her years. "Ladies of the Orphanage, I present to you one of your number, purified, pushed up the Incline, filled with potential. She is now ready to do work, before returning once more to the Orphanage to complete the cycle."

Work. That meant years, decades again of solitude. The cycle, Seg knew, was unforgiving.

"Seg." Her name sounded ceremoniously harsh, like it didn't belong to her at all. "A Plumbess must seek every desert and Plumb it to an oasis as its source, and in this way make civilization. Are you prepared to do this?"

"Yes."

"And so if a man says he is thirsty, you shall say, 'I will turn the valve for you.'"

"I will turn the valve."

"Seg—a Plumbess must seek every habitation and Plumb it to a mire as its drain, and in this way preserve civilization. Are you prepared to do this?"

"Yes."

"And so if a man must defecate, you shall say, 'I will turn the valve for you.'"

"I will turn the valve."

"Seg—neither will you long to spend your life in the oasis or the mire?"

"I will long to spend my life in civilization," Seg replied.

"A Plumbess can only make this commitment if she knows

the difference between right and wrong. And so she must be a competent engineer. Can you produce credentials to this effect?"

"I can." From her bag, Seg removed the diploma that her room had received from the Orphanage a week before—Seg herself had been indisposed. With a bowed head, she handed it to Roc, who read its words before returning it.

"Then you will take this Lead," Roc said as she took a necklace from a nearby orphan. It was a strand of heavy chains centered around an ingot that weighed exactly one kilogram, shaped in the suggestion of a tear or a droplet. While Seg's head remained bowed, Roc strung the necklace around her scarred neck. And although the weight was cumbersome and Roc's hands gnarled with age, she fastened it with surprising dexterity. "And you will be a Plumbess."

Roc then took a stack of papers from another orphan and signed two of the pages. In a quieter voice, she said to Seg, "Sign both of these. One will be for your records, the other will be retained at the Orphanage for either thirty years—when your Certification must be renewed—or your death. Whichever comes first."

Seg signed both copies.

Roc took back the one designated for the Orphanage, then held it for all gathered to see. "A Certified Plumbess," she proclaimed. "May she not re-enter these gates until she's done her work. Now go," she said to the audience. "I need one last word with my ward, so go, all of you."

Whatever it was Roc wanted to say, Seg didn't want to hear it. She was already discounting it wholesale—her thoughts were elsewhere, on where she might go now that she was leaving the only place she'd ever known.

"Seg," Roc said. "Plumbess Seg. Here we finally stand as equals in rank. But you're still very young, and there are things you still won't understand for years to come. What I'm going to tell you is one of those things. You're not going to want to hear it. And for the first time, you won't have to listen to me if you don't want. But I hope you will. I . . . I know what Eck did, and you can't hate her for it."

Seg turned and began walking away. If she didn't have to listen, this was the last thing she would stand around and suffer of her own volition.

"Seg! For the love of the gods, would you just listen to a parting word from your mentor? It's the least you can do after all I've given."

Seg turned around, prepared to argue about how much the Plumbess had given—then she saw the tears in Roc's eyes. When the Plumbess began speaking again, it was with such a soft version of her voice that it almost sounded motherly.

"You can't hate her. You have to find a way to drain your hate, Seg. And not into people. Not into Eck. She loves you, you know. Take your anger and put it somewhere productive. Find a place that needs you. Gods know there are far too many of those out there. Somewhere your skills will be appreciated. Although it pains me to admit, you have plenty of those. Skills."

Strange words to hear from the most bitter, critical person Seg knew. For that reason, she couldn't respond to them, wouldn't respond to them. Instead, she said, "If you're still alive when I return, Plumbess Roc, I'll see you then."

That tightened Roc back up again. The corners of her lips

pulled out severely. She made a jagged movement, turning her back to Seg. Then she went back up the Incline, her steps stricken but not broken by the years.

It was more than what Seg could do. When she also turned to walk away, it felt impossible to move.

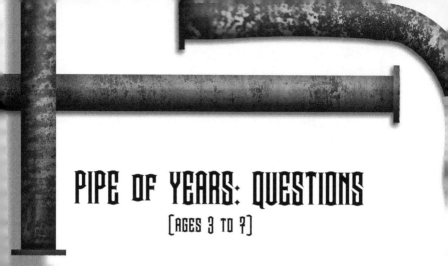

PIPE OF YEARS: QUESTIONS
[AGES 3 TO 7]

FROM WHAT SHE was told, Seg was brought to the Orphanage when she was three years old. Her own memories of her life before, from the perspective of age seven, were fabricated at best. She'd asked Plumbess Roc, the person who'd supposedly brought her here, who her parents were. The Plumbess's response had been, "How should I know?" That had confused Seg into silence for several years.

Whenever she saw a new orphan brought into the Orphanage, however, the old question reasserted itself. It never really went away. The children were always younger than seven, usually half-starved, dirty, and with vacant expressions on their faces. Their hair, always long, was usually tangled in knots. And they were led by a Plumbess who was always quite the opposite: large and domineering, hair in a perfect braid, with a penetrating gaze that Seg never liked returning.

When she was younger, Seg used to ask the new orphans who *their* parents were, perhaps thinking the answers would help unravel her own mystery. But she rarely received cogent responses. One girl in particular had rambled about yarn, a lot about yarn, untying and retying, burning and unburning. Seg avoided her after that. Others would sometimes whisper about violence in vague, impersonal terms that made it clear that they didn't really understand what had happened to them but would also never forget.

On several occasions, Seg had tried to make friends with some of them. There was a redheaded girl in particular—she had glassy, green eyes—that Seg had fallen into a desperate friendship with. Any free time they had, which wasn't terribly much, the two of them would play games in the gardens, games of hide-and-seek and firerock. But the problem with making friends with orphans was that they'd often suddenly disappear just as they'd suddenly arrived, with no trace left of their existence. The little redheaded girl was no exception. Seg asked Roc afterward where the girl went, and the Plumbess said, "How should I know?" And that was that.

The girl hadn't been given an apprenticeship, of that Seg was certain. An apprenticeship was a subtler way to disappear, but just as decisive. Another reason to avoid friendship, especially with children her own age. The orphans, and Seg herself, were destined to be Plumbesses, but the training didn't begin until they were seven years old. When they came of age, they were moved to a different dormitory, and whenever she saw them again—no matter how well they'd known each other, no matter how much time they'd spent toiling together in the gardens—they would ignore her like she was below their dignity. She probably was.

What confused her was why her own apprenticeship hadn't begun. She knew she was seven, even if no one else told her.

She would've asked Roc, but she'd long since learned not to ask the Plumbess any questions of import. So, she waited—impatient, lonely, but resolved.

BEGINNING THE FIRST TIME
[AGE 7]

SEG WAITED UNTIL an hour after the dormitory lights were extinguished and then slipped as silently as she could from her bunk onto the cold stone floor. Although she was mostly confident in her crime—the orphans around her snored soundly, exhausted from the day's hard labor—the consequences of breaking curfew were dire, and she didn't want to take any chances. With exceeding care she opened the room's singular window and climbed into the world beyond.

She did not lower herself to the ground outside. Instead, she grabbed on to the gutter protruding out over the windowsill and prayed it would hold her weight as she pulled herself up onto the dormitory roof. A moment of fear and a brief, flailing effort and she was safely on top.

From there, she did what she came to do: she surveyed the Orphanage.

The Orphanage was a series of concentric circles defined by the Incline. In the daylight, the Incline was a massive cone that was half mountain and half building, dotted all around with terraces and outcroppings and full of gardens, which apparently the Orphanage was famous for. Because Seg wasn't an apprentice or a Plumbess, she wasn't even allowed onto its lowest section, the Bottom of the Incline. In the dark, partially alleviated by a pale moon, the Incline was only a vast silhouette towering upward.

Disappointed, she crossed to the other side of the roof, hoping to see over the Orphanage's outer wall and into the countryside—another place she wasn't allowed to go. A similar darkness presented itself there.

The view hadn't been worth the risk. Frustrated, she collapsed onto the roof, which was probably ill-advised. She held her breath and listened intently for the sounds of people waking below. Only silence.

For four years she'd been confined to the narrow space between the Incline and the Orphanage's outer walls, confined to a few gardens, her dormitory—the one for orphans younger than seven—and several buildings for the servants who worked for the Orphanage. All she wanted was a change, to see *something* else. But if she were ever to climb a roof in daylight, a Plumbess would skin her alive. When her anger finally abated, she climbed back down into the dormitory room, where the orphans continued to snore.

The next morning, the orphans ate their usual communal breakfast and were sent off to work. For about five hours a day they were forced to tend the gardens—digging, planting, watering, pruning. As beautiful as the gardens were, any joy Seg found in them had long since evaporated.

She was elbows deep in a rose bush and thinking blackened thoughts when Plumbess Zag returned to the Orphanage. The Plumbess was having a rough time trying to lead a spindly little girl—her hair probably blonde underneath layers of filth—toward Plumbess Roc, who was overseeing the garden operations. Seg didn't intend to overhear their conversation, but she couldn't very well avoid it either.

Roc spoke first. "It's about damn time. When you told me to wait, I thought you would actually be on your way. But here it is a month later. I'd nearly given you up for dead and moved on."

"It's good to see you again too, Roc." The new Plumbess was much shorter than Roc, softer, stouter. Her white apron, the apron of a Plumbess, was stretched tight in all the same places Roc's found no purchase at all.

"It's been what, twenty-seven years since I left the Orphanage?" she continued. "Any longer and my Certification would've expired. But I found this girl, and I've been travelling the entire month since I left you that message. It's been a difficult month. I found her south of Whales, in a den of snakes—snakes, Roc! And you know they don't care for their young at all, so this one's really doubly an orphan. It was real tricky getting her out of that, and I've been teaching her words and manners ever since. It was just last week I convinced her she had legs. It was pretty slow going before that."

"You know, Zag," Roc said, "there is such a thing as a kid being too far gone."

Seg was curious enough to quickly glance over.

"Nonsense. She's perfect," Zag said. She put a gentle hand on her foundling. The girl flinched a little, but then smiled widely—a huge, unnatural baring of the teeth. Seg shuddered, strangely appalled, and then returned to her work.

"I'll be the judge of that," Roc said.

Whatever happened next, Seg missed it since her head was in the bush. She heard a hiss and an elderly yelping sound, and when she was able to look again she saw Roc recoiled in what almost looked like fear, nursing an injured hand.

"She bit me!"

"We're still working on that. Birds, too. It might be a while before she can behave normally around birds."

"Too far gone, I say. Plumbess Tes will say the same thing—too far gone. Not even a child."

"Well," Plumbess Zag countered, "you see, I've thought about this. And I really think that if she just had a child her age, a better-adjusted one, that she would be able to adapt pretty well. She's fearfully clever, this one. And that's why I asked you to wait. I didn't want to ask you until now—I wanted you to see her first so you knew what you were getting yourself into. You do have a child, right?"

"Yes, she's right over there, ruining that bush," Roc said. "Seg, get over here!"

Seg had been doing such a good job pretending not to overhear that she nearly missed the command, which would have proved fatal. But she recovered and scrambled to where the two Plumbesses and the orphan were gathered. In her haste, she took her garden shears with her, which she held limply in front of her.

"There she is. That little thing, that's it. Didn't think she was anything special, but Plumbess Tes seems to think otherwise. Found her four years ago and have been stuck here ever since. Just my luck, wasting what's left of my life just sitting around here."

Seg's anger flared. Her grip tightened around the shears in her hands, which became the subject of violent imaginings. She didn't ask to be brought to the Orphanage, didn't ask to be left in the care of the worst person she'd ever met. She thought about all the questions Roc refused to answer, and the way the crone criticized her every effort. She very nearly said something damning when Zag spoke instead.

"This *is* your life, Roc. If she's suitable, and you seem to think she is, she's worth those four years and more."

It was the closest thing to reproach Seg had ever heard aimed at a Plumbess. She felt a warm passion for Zag, a warmth so at odds with her feelings toward the other, stiffer, Plumbesses.

"Easy for you to say," Roc replied. "You found yours a month ago. Have you named the creature?"

"Girl," Zag corrected. "And yes. Eck. Her name is Eck."

"Well, you let me know what Plumbess Tes has to say about this Eck of yours. I'm not going to bother making promises to you if she's not even suitable, and I assure you, she's not."

The conversation only deteriorated from there. Then Zag led the orphan girl up the Incline and Roc startled Seg back to work.

Later that night, Seg overheard another of Zag and Roc's conversations—this time, it took place in her dormitory after curfew. Roc, Zag, and a chambermaid were unsuccessfully trying to show the new orphan, definitely blonde after a thorough bath, how to use a bed. Zag would place the girl on the bed, the girl would roll off, slither underneath it, and then hiss at whoever tried to pull her out again.

Roc had originally called the chambermaid in because she didn't want a Plumbess losing a hand, and yet it was always Zag who got on her hands and knees and pulled the squirming girl out to begin the cycle again. They tried to put her on one of the top bunks, but since she slid off that with equal disregard for her wellbeing and landed on her head, they only tried the once.

The bunk in question was one of ten that housed all the orphans under the age of seven, and yet the bunk they picked was right next to Seg.

After several more attempts, during which the Plumbesses would say, "Aren't you tired?" "Stay put already!" "Isn't that comfortable? That's a pillow. For your head. *For your head*," Plumbess Zag finally said, "Maybe it wouldn't hurt if she just slept on the floor after all. She'll figure it out eventually."

"Are you sure she's suitable?" Roc asked. "It's hard to believe that a thing that doesn't understand beds could understand something as complicated as Plumbing."

"Will you continue to doubt me?" Zag responded. "Tes said she's suitable, so you're committed. I wish you'd accept that."

"Fine, fine."

With that the Plumbesses left and the chambermaid extinguished the candles behind them, leaving the orphans in darkness.

Seg didn't sleep very well that night. The snake, Eck, didn't stay under its own bed—it crawled under the beds of the others, one by one. When the snake was under Seg, she held her breath, like maybe she could trick it into thinking the bed was empty.

But the next morning she had a nightmarish recollection—if it was real she didn't know—of the snake twisting up and around the post of her bunk, up under the sheets, and slithering to the bed's center where Seg lay huddled and afraid.

As she ate breakfast, she avoided looking over to where the snake stared, puzzled, at its bowl of porridge. But she could only avoid the snake for so long. Seg blanched at the thought.

Normally the orphans would all go straight from breakfast into some intensive gardening, but Plumbesses Roc and Zag came to get Seg and Eck just as they were dismissed from the table.

"It's time, Seg," Roc said.

"Time, Plumbess?"

"Time to begin your apprenticeship."

"Oh." She'd always thought it would be a pivotal moment in her life, but whether from her poor night's sleep or her aversion to Roc, she mostly felt hollow at the prospect.

"Go get two shovels from the gardening shed. One for you, one for Eck here. Meet us at the gate. Move along."

Seg hurried while she was in sight of the Plumbesses, but once she was out the door and onto the street that skirted the Incline, she adopted a leisurely pace. She wanted to savor the time spent away from the snake. She looked longingly up the Incline—very soon she would be allowed access to the Bottom of the Incline, which would practically be a doubling of her world.

The garden shed revealed itself as a small, white thing—wherever it wasn't covered in green vines—built up against the Orphanage's outer wall. The vines made the doors look hard to open, but since the shed was more level than the earth itself—Plumbesses were obsessed with that kind of thing—the doors swung open easily.

For herself, she picked her favorite shovel. She'd done enough gardening, at the age of seven, to have a favorite shovel. She also had a least favorite shovel, one with a blade so flat that it was like trying to eat soup with a knife. That one she picked for the snake. With both shovels thrown over her shoulder like a Plumbess would carry her plunger, she leisurely strolled toward the gate . . . until she came into sight of Roc, at which point she made a good show of hurrying again.

When she arrived, the Plumbess said, "Insolent little girl. I thought I told you to be quick about it."

"You didn't say that, Plumbess." She didn't know why she said it. It negated the show she'd made, even though the Plumbess had seen through the act. The words were simply out of her mouth before she even considered them.

A tirade was building behind Roc's mottled features; Seg could see it clearly.

Plumbess Zag could see it too. "Why don't we just *move along*, Roc?" she said. "We're losing daylight here."

Somehow, that defused the situation. Seg had never seen that happen before. When Roc was on a rampage, no one could stop her. There were rarely other Plumbesses around, however.

The four of them stepped through the gate.

At first, leaving the Orphanage seemed exciting. It was

what Seg had always thought she wanted—out of her narrow strip of existence, into new vistas. But she quickly tired of the bleak scenery, and it was quite a bit more walking than she was used to. She also had to carry both shovels because the snake would just throw its own and then stare with blank eyes as the Plumbesses chided it. In her growing misery Seg looked once at Eck, hoping to see someone suffering more than herself, but the snake looked like it was *enjoying* the forced march, smiling its terrifying smile and bounding along. Seg only looked the once.

Right before afternoon, Plumbess Zag finally called for a halt. "This is the place," she said. "I can practically smell it. You mind if I explain it to them, Roc? For Eck's sake?"

"By all means," Roc replied, still bitter from hours before.

"This is your first assignment," Zag told the orphans, although she said the words slowly and directed them more at Eck. "There's a village right over there. They don't have running water . . . they don't have water that moves. And they need new outhouses. Somewhere to go to the bathroom in private, Eck. An outhouse is so simple it's not even really Plumbing, it's just a hole in the ground. And that's what you're going to do. You're going to dig a hole in the ground. Do you understand that, Eck? A hole?"

To Seg's amazement, the snake nodded. It was the first instance of supposed communication she'd seen out of it.

"All right. Begin, then."

Seg didn't need to be told twice. If she excelled, if she showed the Plumbesses the true difference in potential between her and the snake, perhaps they wouldn't force her to work with it. She'd heard what they said—they intended to use her as some kind of model of human behavior. That was the last thing she wanted; their single night together had already left its mark. So, she threw her full energy behind the effort and broke the ground hard.

She was surprised again when the snake watched for a few moments and then started digging a hole of its own about five meters away. Seeming satisfied, Plumbess Zag deposited water jugs and bags that probably contained food at the halfway point between the two future outhouses. "We'll leave you to it, then. We'll be right there in the village, and we'll be back at nightfall."

Despite wanting to seem like the picture of diligence, Seg conceded to a groan. Nightfall was about seven hours away. That was more digging than she'd ever done in the gardens. Still, she persisted. She wouldn't be outdone by a snake. She threw shovel after shovel of dirt until even the hardened skin of her hands blistered and bled.

Eventually she entered a sort of trance where nothing mattered to her. By the time she came out of it, she was deep enough that she couldn't see the world outside, and the sky above was already dimming. Thinking to get a drink of water before putting on the final touches, she climbed out, which was a fair struggle.

When she emerged, she realized she was alone.

She had taken it for granted that a person who couldn't speak wouldn't make much noise, but she didn't think Eck would actually *disappear*. She scanned the surrounding trees, but there wasn't a trace of anyone.

There was a hole, though, where Eck had been digging before. Curious, Seg approached it.

It was very narrow, much smaller than Seg's. But it did seem deep. Standing over it, she couldn't see the bottom—it looked like it curved away, into some further darkness. Seg got on her hands and knees and crawled toward the edge, looking deeper. A sudden fear filled her and she was about to back away when a searing pain went through her neck where a monster had latched its teeth.

Her only reaction was to scream. The jaws responded by tightening, and she screamed some more. She was surprised when hands appeared, hands that pulled the jaws apart and let Seg collapse to the ground.

"Oh my, oh my," someone said.

Reflexively, Seg put her hand to the wound. When she pulled it away covered in blood, she proceeded to scream some more.

"Calm down, girl. Calm down. Let me look at it. Yes, yes. It's bad, but it's not that bad. Get up. Come on."

Roc didn't wait for Seg to stand up on her own accord— she grabbed her under the arms and hauled her up. Seg was still whimpering.

There was the snake, a few meters away—and *it* was crying. And what confounded Seg even more was that Zag was *hugging* it, whispering soft words and slowly stroking its back.

"What!" Seg exclaimed. "It—it bit me!"

"Quiet, child, you'll upset her," Zag replied in the same soft tones.

Seg turned to Roc, who only glared back at her. "I suppose," Roc said, "there will have to be a postponement. Let's walk over to the village and see if there's anyone there who can disinfect you and stitch you up. I kind of doubt it, though."

A week later, they returned to the place. In the meantime, wooden buildings had been erected, one over Seg's hole and one over Eck's burrow.

"This is what your work has accomplished," Plumbess Zag said slowly, for Eck. "Now let's walk a little farther."

Past a few trees, a rotten stench welled into existence. "And these are the old outhouses. That's the cycle. A hole is dug, waste gets dumped in, a new hole is dug, the old hole is covered. I've brought you here to complete the cycle. You would've done this part a week ago, but because of the little incident,"—Zag eyed them, Seg and Eck both, with scrutiny—"we had to wait until today. But that's how things go. Pick up your shovels and get to work."

Seg did as she was told: she picked up a shovel and buried the fetid stench of someone else's waste. But this time she didn't let Eck out of her sight.

That night, Seg snuck out of her new dormitory room. She now lived on the Bottom of the Incline, higher than she'd ever been. And even though her hands were tattered and her shoulder bloody, she scaled the side of the building to see what kind of view it would present. She sat on its roof and surveyed the Orphanage.

It was too dark to see.

THE FOUNTAIN, MANOR OF STORMS

FAR AWAY FROM the Orphanage, the same rain started to fail. Eck frowned, a pursing of her thin lips that made them disappear entirely. For ten days she had been following the water wherever it might take her—along swollen streams and drowned moors, past broken mills and despairing peoples. The despairing peoples she consistently avoided.

For ten days, her luck—if that was what it could be called—had held out. It was longer than she could've hoped for, and yet she still hadn't reached her destination. It would be all right though, she thought—she felt close. And if she needed more direction, she could always find it in her dreams, where the rain never ended.

Every once in a while her thoughts touched on Seg and the Orphanage—Seg who she missed, an unsettling feeling. Seg who had driven her out of the Orphanage simply because Eck had told her the truth. But then she remembered that she would've left anyway just a few days later, so things weren't much different than they would've been. And the truth was always worth telling.

So, her mood, more often than not, was subjected to an impervious joy. She splashed in puddles that had plateaued, in streams that would only weaken as the traces of rain slowly faded. When she ran into snakes, she cried out, "Hello," and a few that she especially liked she put into her bag. She swung her plunger in broad arcs, heralding the last of the falling rain, and sang songs that she only knew the melodies to. Until she became hungry again.

Although she'd been raised in captivity, she'd been doing quite well for herself. At the height of the rain, it had been a simple matter to divert a current and then search downstream for whatever animals were surprised by the sudden waters. She ate plenty of drowned rabbits and even a few badgers, which she shared with her bag of snakes. It was so easy that she almost didn't enjoy it. The streams now, though, without the rain to support them, wouldn't be so effective. She would need a new tactic.

Ideas of a hunter were going through her head when she saw the smoke of a chimney. Following the column downward, she saw the stone expanses of some buildings, barely visible behind the beginnings of a valley. A town. Feeling—after ten wandering days—surprising pangs of loneliness, and knowing that people generally had food, she decided to actually visit this one.

She shifted her direction away from the routed waters. She put on her best Plumbess face, one of wisdom and condescension. She threw her plunger over her shoulder the way Zag had done whenever she wanted to make an impression. Eck felt, with confidence, that she looked the part.

And so she arrived at the town of Storm's End. The town and its people were in shambles, destroyed by forces they couldn't control. Even the main road looked like a recently flooded river of stone, its washed-out banks violently cutting the town in two. The shabby people she passed bowed in deference.

One of them addressed her. "Oh, thank the heavens, a Plumbess! It's a miracle! The town, it's a mess!"

By way of conversation, she said, "Good luck with that."

"Won't you," he stumbled in return, "won't you help fix it?"

"Oh," she replied. "No. No I won't."

He frowned.

"The damage is already done, you see," she continued, genuinely unsettled by his frown. "Not much I could do now. If I were here a week ago, I probably could've helped. Not now, though."

His demeanor downcast further.

She didn't understand. No one should be disappointed by the truth, no matter what it might be. Images of Seg struck her again, a look that was far worse than disappointment. It was only the truth.

He could deal with his own problems. And so she didn't mind blithely returning to her own. "Farmer man—"

"I'm the mayor," he replied.

"All right, mayor man, could you tell me if I'm close to the Manor of Storms?"

His downcast demeanor darkened. He was far too emotional for Eck's taste. "Yes, close," he said. "Very close."

"That's wonderful! Could you give me an orphan, then?"

"You intend to be their Plumbess? The Plumbess of the Manor of Storms?"

"I do."

He took a moment to consider. "On one condition," he said. "I'll get you an orphan if you remind Pipe Lord Marcus of his responsibility to his vassals." He made a broad gesture encompassing the broken town.

Eck was displeased. She shouldn't have to barter for an orphan. If she asked, an orphan would be given—it was a tradition that stretched back for centuries. And yet he was only asking for words in return, and words were easy enough. "Responsibility to his vassals," she repeated slowly. "Yes, I can do this. For one orphan, please."

"I'll have it arranged, then," he said, and walked away.

Eck quickly grew bored. This orphan must not have been easily accessible, must have been off in the countryside or something unfortunate like that. To pass the time, she began to fix the eaves of a building that struck her fancy.

A little after she began, a portly woman came running out, saying, "What on earth are you doing to my house! Hasn't it suffered enough, you, you—" But then she saw Eck, and her protective anger immediately faltered. "Plumbess," she whispered. "I apologize. I didn't mean anything by it."

"Okay," Eck said. Then she stood there motionless as the lady watched her from the sunken porch.

"I'll just . . . I'll just be inside, I guess," the lady said.

Eck nodded and watched her leave before returning to

what she was doing. The gutters of the house were full of compacted leaves, fetid and decaying.

"No wonder this town couldn't handle the storm," she said to her bag of snakes. Even her plunger was overwhelmed by the magnitude of the blockage. She pulled out her drain auger, which she'd always had a special affinity for, and cleared out a majority of one of the pipes. Then, as a matter of curiosity, she pulled one of the snakes out of her bag, whispered instructions to it, and dropped it down the pipe to see if it would finish the job.

She was in the middle of this, straddling the eaves between the one building and the next, when the mayor man finally returned with the orphan. She didn't bother finishing what she was doing—she put away her drain auger, called back her snake, and rejoined the mayor man on the ground. His eyes, a little wide, were staring at her bag, where she had replaced the snake.

Eck got her first good look at the orphan, and was confused by what she saw. "Is something wrong with it?" she asked.

"What do you mean?"

"Its hair is short, for one. And its face is shaped differently. Not wearing any shoes either." The last part confused Eck—she thought people needed shoes.

"He's a boy, if that's what you mean. A poor one. I apologize, but he's the only orphan we've got."

"A boy orphan? And you didn't eat it?"

"I . . . we don't really eat *any* orphans around here, boy or girl."

"Hmm. Okay. Does it know what to do?"

"I haven't told him anything yet."

Eck got down on her knees so she could look the orphan boy in the face. It didn't return her gaze. It seemed defective. She pulled off her left glove. "It's rather simple, orphan boy. You're going to go to the Manor of Storms, and when you see Pipe Lord Marcus you're going to say, 'A Plumbess would be beneficial. I recommend Plumbess Eck.' Plumbess Eck, that's my name. Give this to him, this glove. Take it already. And then you'll bring him back here, to this place, that's the most important part. Bring him back here. Understood?"

The orphan boy stared dazedly at the glove that she'd finally managed to impress into its hands.

"Can you get it to move, mayor man?" she implored. "I'd like for this interaction to be over."

"Get along, boy!" he yelled, and the boy got along.

Eck watched as it ran, watched until it disappeared around a ruined warehouse at the end of the street.

"Now that that's out of the way," she said to the mayor man, "is there something I could eat? I'm very hungry."

"Oh, of course," he said. "This way."

He led her to an inn that showed obvious signs of ad hoc repair. The repairs, though, had clearly missed the mark. One corner of the foundation in particular sagged heavily, and the smell of mold was already in the air.

Eck said, "Your people, they aren't very good at fixing things. Are they not trained?"

For some reason he didn't answer her. Instead, he pointed at a chair by a table and said, "If you sit there, I'll have food out to you shortly."

Happy to be obedient if it meant food, Eck sat as suggested. Time went by. She smelled food on the horizon—they were cooking it, which was probably good. That was the way humans did it, and she could stand to be more human. Even though Zag always talked about how beneficial it was to cook things, Eck had done without on her travels. Too much waiting. But she was already waiting anyway.

When they finally brought it out, it turned out to be a weak soup, mostly onion. But she reassured herself in the same way—that it was something humans should eat, and therefore she should too. So she said thank you, because that was the proper thing to do, and drained her bowl.

The mayor man, in the meantime, had taken a seat across the room. He stared at her in random intervals. It felt unusual, but did her no harm. More time went by, too much time. She was starting to become firmly convinced that the orphan was in fact defective when she heard the unmistakable sounds of hooves on the wet ground outside. The Pipe Lord. She stood up and walked outside.

Six black horses, glossy and terrifying, pulled a magnificent carriage of the same color. Gold piping rimmed the carriage, augmenting its splendor. Eck noticed, to her dissatisfaction, that the piping couldn't possibly be of any utility. Perhaps the Pipe Lord would let her fix that.

A liveryman jumped from the top of the carriage to the ground, where he became temporarily mired. But eventually he managed to open the door of the carriage, exposing its plush red-velvet core.

A man, a beautiful man, disgorged himself from the carriage interior. As he descended onto the mud-covered ground, he placed his pointed boots with care. His face, a gleaming smile, was directed unequivocally at Eck. He walked to meet her, his left hand extended. The bare skin of their left hands touched, for a moment, before he returned Eck her glove, which she immediately put back on.

"I was beginning to fear that I would live and die without ever having you by my side, dear Plumbess Eck," he said. "And yet here you are, performing a genuine Service Call. I didn't take you to be one for formalities when I met you at the Orphanage."

"If I am to be a Plumbess, then I will do it properly," Eck replied.

"In that case," he said, "may I see your Certification, so that I might draw up a Contract of Work?"

"Not possible," she said a little overly loud. When she was embarrassed, she tended to shout.

He only laughed, though. "For someone who has decided to do things properly, you've certainly skipped over some of the more important conventions. No matter, though. Come along—allow me to get you out of this mess."

That reminded Eck. She glanced over at the mayor man, who had been watching their conversation from the balcony of the inn. "I made an exchange for the orphan. The mayor man wanted me to remind you of . . . of your responsibility to your vassals, yes."

The Pipe Lord looked over to where the mayor man was suddenly struggling with the handle to the inn's front door, which of course didn't work properly. "He did, did he? Well, consider me reminded. Let's be on our way."

Glad to be discharged of her obligation, Eck complied. Once they were settled, the horses set in motion and the carriage bounded along.

Eck asked, "I'm not too late, then? I was afraid another Plumbess would come and take the position you offered. I came as soon as I could."

For whatever reason, a Pipe Lord was only allowed to have one Plumbess. Eck didn't understand it—in her experience, Plumbesses could always accomplish more together than they could on their own.

"Oh, they came. The Manor of Storms is a coveted position, after all. But I turned them all down. Didn't even answer their Service Calls. I even had one ejected from the Manor when she came anyway. You are the only Plumbess for me."

Eck smiled. It was nearly impossible for her to hide her emotions, especially when she succeeded at something. She'd spent nearly ten days following the rain, and she'd ended up exactly where she intended to be.

The Pipe Lord said, after a while, "If I recall correctly, you should've been close to your Certification. May I enquire?"

"Enquire what?" she asked, always at a loss with social vagueness.

"Enquire why it was that you weren't Certified."

The memory clouded Eck's happiness for a moment, like a cirrus across the sun. "My mentor died during the storm. And Seg, she made me leave the Orphanage." She left it at that.

"My condolences," he said.

Out the window, dirty and shiftless farmers stood and watched the carriage as it rolled by. She asked, "Do you own all of these people?"

"Own them?" He laughed. "No, I don't own them. I own the land they work on, though. The minerals, the water. I own the sky above them. And I own half of what they produce. So no, I don't own *them*, but I do own almost everything that they are. Almost everything."

He paused. "Speaking of what they make, it seems that this year's harvest has been ruined. But the Manor's gardens, those will provide us enough food to last until next year's harvest. Acres and acres covered in glass, so they were spared the rain. Watered by some of the most impressive Plumbing known to man. You'll love them, I'm sure."

They did sound lovely. Back at the Orphanage, the gardens were the place Eck had felt most comfortable, most at home. She asked, "I'll have somewhere to live, right? And food?"

He laughed again; he laughed a lot. "I don't know what you think you've signed up for, Plumbess, but yes—the most lavish furnishings and food the entire world over. Anything you need, it's all yours."

That was reassuring enough for Eck. She couldn't care less about lavish things, but food and a place to live—those were good.

The carriage emerged from the valley and suddenly they had a full view of the land beyond. Dominating its center was a building unlike anything Eck had ever seen. She'd heard the metaphor "touch the sky" before, spoken of tall things—she actively catalogued metaphors to combat her difficulty with them. It made little sense, this particular metaphor, since the sky started right above the ground, and surface area should be more important than height, as far as touching went. But this building, it literally touched the sky. It penetrated it fully—a permanent storm loomed over it, bound in place by metal and engineering. Lightning often struck as she watched, as if the sky was upset by the violation.

The pipework was amazing—it interlaced, extended, captured the very moisture from the sky. It resembled a spider web, and Eck had a certain respect for spiders. The crystal surfaces of the building, the gardens that the Pipe Lord had spoken of, looked like flies caught in its snare.

As above, so below. There was a river—meandering on its innocent way to the ocean—that the Manor surprised and swallowed whole. Eck's serpentine instincts flared up, excited. "So much to work with," she said in awe. "A river and the sky."

"I knew you'd like it," the Pipe Lord replied.

When they got closer, Eck felt a moment of fear. The building, opening up around them, resembled to her a larger creature, and every part of her wanted to resist entering its maw. But then the jaws closed and she was left without a choice—copper, crystal, and human concerns enclosed them on all sides.

The carriage drew to a stop. She heard the liveryman dismount, and then the door opened and she was overwhelmed by the smells of water and metal and oil and everything in between. The Pipe Lord got out first and helped her to disembark.

"I wanted to show you the Fountain first," he said.

It was unlike any Plumbing she had ever seen. There were waterfalls that fell up instead of down; streams that intricately intertwined and yet emerged distinct; pools suspended in midair, spilling but constantly refilled. If someone had told her before that such things could be done, she would've denied it, and with certainty.

"Welcome," Pipe Lord Marcus said, "to the Manor of Storms."

THE GRAVE, HOPE SPRINGS

WHEN SEG CHOSE a direction to distance herself from the Orphanage with, it was the direction opposite the fleeing rain. Still, it took two days of walking before the clouds dissipated and revealed the sun again.

Although her shirt was linen, her sweat pooled beneath it anyway. So much walking caused her ankles to chafe on her rubber boots. And her Lead: the heavy chains of the necklace rubbed her skin raw, especially where it crossed the scar Eck had given her. In such a state of discomfort, it was difficult for her to keep a positive attitude.

It didn't help that her food had dried up, coincidentally or not, at the same time the sun reappeared. To replenish, she began stopping at villages and small towns, which by tradition would exchange food for small favors from a Plumbess. The people were more than delighted to see her, although she never reciprocated any of their smiles or graciousness.

She stopped leaks, unclogged toilets, repaired dams, and assisted the digestion of the elderly. Sometimes she could get away with less physical work, like predicting the weather or simply giving gardening advice. She'd done plenty of gardening.

At one village she delivered a baby, an expertise of hers. The local midwife watched the whole time with jealousy in her eyes. Seg didn't care. Humans, in the final appraisal, were nothing more than complicated pipes, and Seg reveled in the complexity. She labored for three hours and was rewarded with a little girl. For Seg's efforts, the mother tried to name the girl after her.

In return, Seg gave her anger. "A three-letter name is the name of an orphan. Promise me right now that you will take care of her."

The mother, surprised by Seg's severity, nodded.

And she moved on. The farther she travelled, the drier the world became. Soon, all of the favors she traded for food had to do with sourcing water—her plunger could be used as a dowsing rod. She would lead a group of elders to some lost aquifer and admonish them as if they'd already wronged it.

"This water, this source, which has hidden so well from you for so long, is to be used sparingly. Only for drinking, or for cleaning when sanitation is necessary. If you don't abide by this principle, it could be the last water your village ever knows."

The elders would nod, but Seg got the impression that they only listened because she was a Plumbess. So deep in the countryside, Plumbesses were treated with an almost superstitious reverence. But as long as they respected the water, Seg didn't care why.

One day, Seg was sewing a copper pipe together with needle and thread in exchange for a sandwich when the man she was helping said to her, "It'll be good to have a Plumbess at Hope Springs again. More than good—practically a miracle. It's been over twenty years, and I know that Pipe Lord Carral could use the help. *We* could use the help. Our livestock is dying off at a rate we can't ignore."

"Hope Springs? Pipe Lord Carral?"

He looked at her for a moment, not believing the question in her voice. "You came from the west, did you not? The only thing further east of here is Hope Springs—otherwise it's just the desert. Just the desert. You were going to this place, yes?"

"I was merely wandering," she said.

"Not possible," he replied. "There's no paths around here—wandering would be certain death. If you'd missed this village by just a kilometer north or south, you'd be wandering in the desert until you die. You're on your way to Hope Springs. It's only a few kilometers due east of here."

Seg didn't argue with him. She could recognize the strings of fate when they wound themselves around her. She was on her way to Hope Springs. It was good to know.

"Yes, Hope Springs," she said. "And if it's as close as you say, perhaps I can return at some point to help your village. But first things first. I'll need to have a Service Call performed. Do you have an orphan that would be suitable for the task?"

"I know just the one," he said, already standing up. "I'll be right back, Plumbess."

She made her last stitches, then tied the thread off. She took one last look at the seam—not her best work—and then opened the valve upstream of the pipe. It quickly filled with precious water, and the stitches held. "Good enough," she told the pipe, and put her materials away.

Since she would be presenting herself to a Pipe Lord, she decided it would be best to look the part of a Plumbess. She found a mirror and took the first look at herself since she'd left the Orphanage.

Her hair cascaded wildly to her waist, a jumbled mess. Weeks of sun had done nothing to change her otherworldly pallor, which she thought strange. The whole side of her neck was crusted with blood, centered around where her Lead crossed her scar. Against her inclination, she took some water from the pipe she'd fixed and dabbed it away. Then she took a pipe brush from her bag and worked at her hair until it fell into black streams of luster.

The man returned with the promised orphan. It was a girl, six or seven, who looked far healthier than any orphan Seg had ever seen. She wore an excited expression on her face. Seg felt she knew the reason, and hated it.

"Have you come to take me away, Plumbess?" the orphan asked. "I knew this day would come! I've prayed every day for as long as I can remember, and—"

"No," Seg said, cutting into the girl's hope like a knife. She hated to do it, but it had to be done. "I'm sorry, but that's not why I'm here."

The girl's face immediately clouded over. Seg lowered herself to her knees so she could speak to her face-to-face.

"Could you tell me what your name is?" Seg asked.

"Rachel." A single tear fell down the left side of her face.

"Rachel. That's the name of a little girl who is loved. I can tell—I can see just by looking at you that someone cares about you very much. That's more than most any girl at the Orphanage has, and I want you to know that. If you left, if I took you away, that person would be very sad. You don't want that, do you?"

The girl shook her head, disrupting the flow of the tear.

"Good. In that case, I'd like to ask you a favor. Do you know what a Service Call is?"

"I think so."

"Well, I'll explain it anyway, just in case. It's not that complicated—the hardest part is that you'll have to do it alone, but I believe in you. You're going to take this"—she peeled the glove off her left hand—"and you'll go to Hope Springs. You'll tell anyone who listens that you've found a leak, and when they see this glove they'll take you straight to the Pipe Lord. To him you will say, 'It would be beneficial to call a Plumbess. I recommend Plumbess Seg.' And then he'll bring you back here. Understood?"

"I have to find a leak?" the girl asked. Her eyes were locked on the glove, black and sterile, in her hand.

"No. Strangely enough, that's the least important part. You just have to say that you did, or that you found something else that a Plumbess might fix. I prefer a leak."

"Okay. I can do that."

"I'll walk with you as far as the edge of the city, but I can't go farther than that. Will you show me the way?"

The girl nodded, and they walked off. When they reached the edge of the city, Seg stayed behind, but she continued watching until the girl disappeared in the distance. Because the ground was incredibly flat and without vegetation, that took a considerable amount of time. When Seg finally moved again, her joints only worked stiffly.

She wouldn't have time to do anything substantial to help the village, but there was no reason she couldn't take a brief survey of it. She took out her plunger and used it to strike the ground while she listened, as she'd seen Zag do so many times before. She imitated the woman more than she cared to admit. And so she circumnavigated the village, Plumbing its depths like a boat looking to moor.

Although it was impossible to know for certain what lay below, she got a good, bleak impression. There was one pipe in particular, extraordinarily hollow, that seemed in one direction to go toward Hope Springs. Curious, she followed it the other direction, into the center of the village.

It led her to a large fountain in the middle of a plaza, completely dry. She could make out the marks of previous waterlines, but they had turned into myths. With a deep sense of shame, she sat on its lip and waited as the sun sank toward the horizon.

The man from before found her there several hours later. He said to her, "That's from Hope Springs. It used to be full, years ago."

"I know," she said.

He sat down next to her and looked longingly into the depths of the bowl. "It's strange how dry things can get."

"Shouldn't the girl be back by now? You said it was only a few kilometers, right?"

"She'll be fine."

"If she's still not here in an hour, I'm going to go find her, Service Call be damned."

It didn't come to that. A few minutes later, two figures appeared in the distance. Seg was confused since she had expected a carriage, but at least her concern fled—one of the shapes was smaller, and certainly the orphan. The other looked like an old man. She walked out to meet them, leaving the village behind. When the other figure resolved itself, she couldn't believe what she was seeing—golden epaulettes on a man's shoulders. It was a Pipe Lord, walking through the desert to meet her.

She heard the orphan say, "That's her, right there. The Plumbess."

"Very good," he mumbled. "Very good."

When they were close, the Pipe Lord extended his right hand, demanding an embrace.

Seg hesitated.

"Oh, that's right," he said, and switched it for his left.

This she accepted. "My glove?" she asked. He was supposed to return her glove to her.

"I'm afraid," he mumbled, patting the pockets on his thighs and chest, "that I've misplaced it. No glove, no."

Moderately annoyed, Seg said, "No matter." She pulled a new one out of her bag and put it on. "More importantly, where is your carriage?"

"I'm afraid . . . " he repeated, and descended into a mumbling so low that it was unintelligible except for the occasional *k* sound.

She interrupted him, or at least she would have if he were speaking words. "Am I to presume, then, that you aren't in a position to draw up a proper Contract of Work?"

That flared up his indignation, although he looked as if he wasn't well versed in its use. "Now see here, Mrs. Plumbess. The circumstances are regrettable—I'm an old man walking in a desert—but we have to make the best of them, right? There's plenty to be excited about, isn't there? A Plumbess, after all this time. Plumbess Mar, rest her soul, certainly left the place in quite the disarray. Wonderful woman, terrible mess."

The name, Mar, caused Seg a considerable shock. Out of all the Pipe Lords she could've made her way to—and there were thirty-four of them, the title passed down paternally generation after generation—she'd found the one Plumbess Mar had served. Zag's mentor. Seg had heard so many stories about Mar that she felt she practically knew her. Stories from Zag . . . yet another thing tying her to her painful past. She felt the strings of fate draw tighter.

Rather than deal with her past, she turned to the orphan, thanked her for her service, and sent her back home. She noticed, as she watched the girl go, that the Pipe Lord wouldn't look at the village. Some sort of shame branded him too.

He grunted and said, "Might as well be on our way, don't you think?"

"Let's," she said.

After fifteen minutes of walking, they came across a broken carriage stranded in a wasteland of dryness. It was lying on the scattered remains of a full set of wheels in a way that suggested they had disintegrated simultaneously. Two men were working feverishly to fix them, and two horses wandered in the distance looking for a shrub to eat—they wouldn't find one.

"So you did have a carriage," she said to the Pipe Lord.

"I told you as much before."

"No you didn't."

One of the men saw them approach and came to greet them. He bowed for the Plumbess and Pipe Lord equally. "Pleasure to meet you, Plumbess. Should be done very soon, Pipe Lord. Not the best of fixes, but it should at least get us back to the Springs. I hope."

"Hope is all you need!" the Pipe Lord exclaimed, suddenly jovial. "Let us into the carriage. I've done enough walking for one day, and it'll be nice to at least end this ordeal properly."

It was obvious that the lackey was neither carpenter or livery-man by trade. He awkwardly lowered the stairs to the carriage and held the door.

Inside, Seg was confronted by the confined smell of the Pipe Lord, which she'd sensed before but not in force. It was a dark mustiness, a dry rot that had probably set in decades ago. It was hard to deal with, but she did her best. She took a seat directly by the window and watched as the man outside ran to get the horses, who scattered at his approach.

She made the mistake of thinking everything was resolved, she said, "I suppose this means we can draw up the Contract of Work?" She proffered her Certification, which she'd kept ready in her bag.

"I'm afraid—"

"Fine!" she snapped, cutting him off immediately this time. After that, she dropped the issue entirely.

Another twenty minutes went by before the horses were gathered, harnessed, and set in motion. The new wheels groaned loudly, as if they might soon give up the same ghost as their predecessors.

The Pipe Lord then began speaking, as if continuing some conversation from before. " . . . He'll help you with that, of course. Baron Gregor. You'll like him, he's a good lad. Good breeding, that always goes far, don't you think?"

Seg, an orphan, didn't reply. The mustiness inside the carriage grew, until she feared she wouldn't be able to breathe. She checked the window for a clasp to open it, but of course there wasn't one. She was seriously contemplating getting out and walking the rest of the way when the Pipe Lord suddenly rattled on the front wall of the carriage with a stick he had. "Stop here, lad! The monument, the grave, stop at the grave! The lady Plumbess, she'll want to see it."

The carriage drew to a stop. She realized, as she hadn't before in her panic, that they were near some buildings. The door of the carriage opened, blinding her in its sudden light. Soon, her eyes adjusted and she found herself just inside the gates of a small town, next to an enormous statue.

It was the statue of a Plumbess, her plunger stuck resolutely into the ground. It reminded her terribly of a dream she'd had of Zag, another Plumbess frozen in stone, another silent façade with no real answers to offer her. She followed the Pipe Lord anyway, who walked up to a plaque and large basin that stood in front of the statue. The basin was, of course, dry, and discolored by the sun and time.

"I was lucky," he told Seg as they stood there. "Some Pipe Lords, they live and die without ever once having a Plumbess by their side. More Pipe Lords than Plumbesses, they say. But I've been blessed. I had Plumbess Mar. Forty years ago, back when I was an ambitious young lad with more pipe than I knew what to do with. He-he. She helped me . . . " His eyes glazed over in aged reverie.

Seg looked past the statue, at the dying town behind it. Jagged pipes stuck out in random directions everywhere she looked. The air was dry, moistureless—the smell she'd thought idiosyncratic to the Pipe Lord seemed to be everywhere. It would be a harder task than any she'd undertaken, making the place livable.

"If there's work to be done, I'd rather be taken there than here," she said.

"You heard the Plumbess, lad!" the Pipe Lord yelled at his lackey, all excitement again. "Back in the carriage! Onward!"

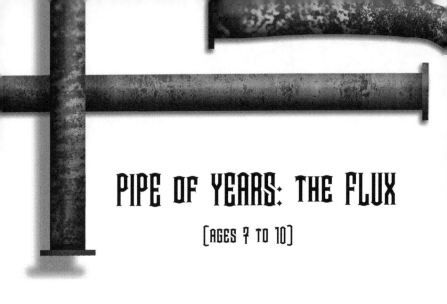

PIPE OF YEARS: THE FLUX

[AGES 7 TO 10]

SEG'S INITIAL DISAPPOINTMENT with her apprenticeship grew into a thriving ecosystem. The sights from the Bottom of the Incline were essentially the same as the sights below, the same food was served in the dining hall, and even her new dormitory, designated for apprentices, had about the same number of children in it—just a little older. Eck somehow slept the same distance from her as before. Seg would stay up late at night, compulsively stroking the scar on her neck—long since healed over—and listening to the girl's hissing snores. She thought about how close she'd been to dying, and how no one really cared.

Although Seg still spent most of her time gardening, she also spent at least a few hours each day in Roc's workshop, learning the basics of Plumbing. It was a long time before she was trusted with anything better than a shovel. Instead, the old Plumbess stacked up books for her—formulas to work out, theorems to memorize. Roc focused for the longest time on geometrical considerations and trigonometry, and especially the way Seg held her pen, which Roc arbitrarily hated.

Then came the fundamental concepts of flow—water pressure and frictional losses—and the importance of pitch, the necessary tilt of a pipe that allowed water to gravity-drain.

"Two fingers, one arm," Roc explained. "For every arm's length of pipe, it should descend at least two fingers in height. You know what an arm is, right?"

It was one of Roc's favorite jokes, pretending like Seg didn't know anything about the most everyday of objects. Roc loved it because she knew Seg hated it—Seg hated it because there *was* an apprentice who probably didn't know what an arm was, a difficulty Seg had to deal with on a daily basis.

Eck, Seg was confident, only understood about a tenth of what was said to her, whether about Plumbing or gardening or how to treat people. She hissed at everyone and bit several people who got too close to her anyway, although none so severely as she'd bitten Seg. She rarely did much gardening since she was apparently deathly afraid of the nesting birds. And yet Zag still encouraged her with kind words and a pat on the back. Anyone else and Eck would've bitten them for touching her—but not Zag.

Seg did her best to focus on her own education. She studied long and often, in sickness and in health. When she could finally reproduce and perform all the requisite calculations to Roc's absurd standard, Roc allowed her to work with some real metal: copper. She learned how to weld compatible metals with fire and solder incompatible ones with flux. And she built.

But despite Seg's best efforts, Roc responded to everything with criticism. She would take a pipe in her hand, glare at it for a moment like it insulted her personally, and then break it over the nearest object. "If it was soldered properly, it wouldn't break like that," she'd say.

It wouldn't have bothered Seg so much if she didn't know that Roc was right. So, she returned to the flux and tried again.

WOOD SHOWERS
[AGE 10]

ONE DAY, SEG entered Roc's workshop and none of the materials were there—no formulas on the blackboard, no metal or tools on the workbench. The Plumbess was there, but she didn't look up as Seg entered. She was reading some old letter written in Plumbess code, which Seg hadn't been taught to read yet. Fearing that the Plumbess had truly given up on her after so many threats to do so, Seg prepared for the worst.

Then Roc said, "Zag seems to think the two of you are ready for the next challenge. You know I have my doubts, but for some reason the decision isn't mine."

The bent Plumbess stood, and was hardly taller for it. She folded the letter, then looked down at Seg. "Off to the woods again. Let's go," she said, and immediately set off.

Without looking back to see if Seg followed, the Plumbess continued to talk. "Those outhouses you dug—and don't start crying about your little scratch again, girl, I've heard enough about it—those weren't even Plumbing. No pipe, no pressure, no purpose. Just holes in the ground for people to shit in and pretend it's not offensive to humanity. Real Plumbing doesn't smell, and not because it covers everything with fancy odors, with roses or some nonsense like that to deaden the senses. Roses aren't for toilets. No, it doesn't smell because there's nothing *to* smell—the shit's off where smells can't be smelled, except by the Plumbesses who have to come back and fix it years later because no one uses pipes right. But that's a lesson for another day. Today is about what Plumbing *should* be, about building and design. Plumbing is sanitary, not just some shit hole. Plumbing transforms, conveys.

"So, this time you're going to get a little closer to the real thing. You're going to build a shower out in the middle of the woods, where no one can be injured by your incompetence. I don't have to explain a shower to you, do I, foul girl? You know at least that much, as dull-witted as you are? You have to find a proper source, water from somewhere that won't be missed. That's the first part.

"And then you have to send the water up the Incline so it can do some useful work—the shower itself. It has to be the kind of thing that can clean a person. And not only that, but it must be the user interface—it must provide ways for the person to choose what they want from it, but also intuitive enough that they can make that choice without dying. Since there's hot water involved here, you can bet someone will find a way to kill themselves. I've seen people burned, child, disfigured much worse than your little scar, and by something as simple as hot water. Not to be underestimated. Intuitive, effective, and safe cleaning—that's the second part of a shower, but by no means the most important.

"And finally, you have to take the dirty water and send it down the drain, to some Orphanage where it has to put up with insubordinate children for the rest of its life. Put it somewhere it won't do harm. You can't just put it back where you got it, not without cleaning it up first, otherwise you'll just be showering in your own filth. Remember pitch, girl, two fingers per arm."

From there the Plumbess descended into a barrage of insults interspersed with Plumbing rules of thumb. The breadth and diversity of insults betrayed the Plumbess's true passion, and Seg was already familiar with the tenets of Plumbing after so many months of reading books that explained it better.

"Did you get all that?" Roc finally asked, after speaking endless volumes.

"Sure," Seg said.

"Any questions?"

"Will I have flux?"

The Plumbess just snorted.

Seg should've known not to ask anything else, but she was curious. "Will the villagers use my shower?" she asked. She was thinking about the outhouses and the people at the receiving end of her work.

"What was that, girl?"

"Will the villagers use my shower?" she repeated, quieter the second time.

"Ha! You think you're going to build something useful, girl? With what little you know? I can guarantee you that it won't even turn on. If this was about real, working showers, we might as well turn around now. You know how useless you are. No, no one will use your shower, and that's a good thing.

Although hopefully at the very least it breaks that pride of yours. That would be useful."

Seg only held her head higher—if it was a challenge, then she'd make the best shower the old witch had ever seen.

"Now, any last wrong questions to ask, girl? Last chance."

Seg realized with surprise that they'd already arrived—for the first half of the walk she'd been drowned by Roc's words, which required so much filtering to make potable, and for the second half she'd been distracted by her growing anger.

They were in a clearing—enormous trees touched the sky around them, connecting sky and earth. Eck and Zag were already there as well, next to two conspicuous and large boxes in the clearing's center. Zag was kneeling down and talking to Eck face-to-face, probably giving the snake the same explanation Roc had given her but in more humane terms.

When Zag saw them arrive, she stood up. "I'm glad you're late," she said. "I do believe Eck nearly understands what we're doing here, but I'm sure that having Seg as a role model will still be very helpful. Seg knows what's expected of her?"

"I've told her," Roc replied. "Gods know what she actually retained."

"Now, Roc, she's a very smart girl. I have nothing but faith. Anyway, do you both see these boxes? They have everything you should need. If you think you need something else, you're probably overthinking it, and you should try to solve the problem a different way. Just make the best shower you can. So, if you're both clear on the expectations, or at least you, Seg, then we should be off. We'll be back in the morning to see what you've done. Do you hear that, Eck? *I will see you tomorrow.* Okay? Say okay."

"Okay," Eck said.

And with that, the Plumbesses left. Seg went straight to her box and took a thorough inventory of her supplies. Eck, in the meantime, just stared at her with her wide, unblinking eyes. After a few minutes, Seg lost her composure. With a copper pipe and a well-tempered anger, she struck the side of her box. The pipe bent, becoming useless.

"Stop staring at me!" she yelled at Eck. "Go do your own work! Do you think it's fair that I do all the hard parts and you just copy me and get the same amount of credit? Really you'll get more credit, because Zag will love whatever *you* do. But you're going to find out that this is more difficult than digging a hole, snake. This is Plumbing. Go!"

The snake seemed to take the strong hint—she went to her own box, and Seg was able to focus better. She took an armful of everything she thought she'd need and set out without the intention of coming back—even though it would've been easier to scout a location and then return for the materials, she didn't want to give Eck an opportunity to follow her. Whatever the Plumbesses wanted, the snake would build her own shower.

Seg delved deeper and deeper into the forest, keeping a constant eye out for good locations. She had a lot of practical thoughts—as many streams as she passed, she stopped at none of them. Streams were too changeable, unreliable. She needed a constant source. She didn't have the time or resources to bury her pipes; she'd have to run them along the ground or through the branches. Where would she put the drain?

She started with trying to find a source and wasted far too much time on one pond in particular, nestled in a gentle corner of the woods. Although small, it was filled with life, with frogs and ducks and more insects than she could count. She stared at it for hours, and every time a frog croaked or a duck alighted she grew more and more diffident. Not because frog water would make for a poor shower—she was in the middle of the woods and would take what she could get—but because the pond was small and she could vividly imagine that, after just a single shower, all the frogs would dry to dust and the ducks would choke on their remains. Eventually she stood up, horrified.

The pipes in her arms got heavier the farther she walked. But by luck, or a random impulse, or perhaps even intuition—later on and thinking back, she could've sworn the water had *called* to her—her search ended just as it was getting dark. Obscured by heavy brush was the narrow entrance of a cave. She deposited her armload and went inside.

If she wasn't so small, she never would've reached the end. More than once she pushed herself through cracks she wasn't confident she'd return from until finally she reached an enormous crystalline expanse of water deep underground. It was cold to the touch; it was cleanliness manifest and everything she needed.

Encouraged by her discovery, she returned outside to establish a quick plan, and from there she immersed herself in her work.

She nearly drowned in the lake while routing copper pipes to its heart. The mouth of the cave, hidden as it was behind the brush, was the perfect place for a discreet shower. By the light of the stars she fashioned a showerhead and mounted it directly into the face of the stone, using rivets she managed to chisel in.

Because the lake was lower than her showerhead, she couldn't rely on gravity to make her shower work. So she built a little peristaltic pump that would need to be hand-cranked to make the water flow. It was the best she could do.

"Two fingers, one arm," she whispered to herself as she entered the last stage of her design. "Two fingers, one arm."

Only after committing herself so heavily and nearly reaching the point of exhaustion did she realize that she had a draining problem. The cave mouth, with respect to its surroundings, was at a considerable low point. To run a drain out of it would require drilling through six meters of solid rock, which wasn't an option. The shower could only possibly drain into itself.

In the end she settled for a small hole dug into the corner of the shower with a narrow trench leading up to it. It wouldn't be very good, but at that point she was too tired to do better. Lying at the foot of her shower, staring into the stars above, she fell asleep.

She woke to the most unpleasant sound she could think of: Roc's voice. "Get up, girl! Time to be judged."

The two Plumbesses towered over her. Eck was there too, standing awkwardly at a distance.

Seg stood up. With all four of them inside, the outdoor shower felt rather crowded. "This is it?" Roc said, inspecting it up and down. "Where does this go?" she asked Zag, and indicated the pipe leading up to the showerhead.

Zag struck the pipe, delicately but firmly, with her plunger. She turned her head to listen. "An underground lake," she finally said. "Down in this cave. A very good find, I'd say."

"Say what you want," Roc replied. "This is laughable."

She had Seg's peristaltic pump in her hand, and gave it a few cranks. Drops of water appeared at the showerhead.

"It's a passable solution, Roc. What did you expect her to do? This, on the other hand, this I agree should've been thought out a little better."

The Plumbesses were both looking at her drain, like she knew they would. Roc said, "If you took a real shower in here, girl, you'd drown yourself. It's a safety hazard."

"But it would be a clean death, and that's mostly the point," Zag said in Seg's defense. "You understand though, Seg, that this doesn't work, right?"

"Yes, Plumbess."

"That's good, that's all that matters. We're learning, that's what we're here for. And we're in the woods, Roc, not some city with utilities. I think we've said enough here. Let's find Eck's. Eck, where did you build your shower?"

She asked Eck multiple times, but the best answer she got was "leaf." So instead, the Plumbesses turned to Seg. "Did you see where she built it, Seg?"

"No, the last place I saw her was where you left us. Where did you find her this morning?"

"With you."

An uncontrollable shiver went up and down Seg's spine. How had Eck found her? And how long had she been there, lurking? Seg tried to recall if she'd had any nightmares, but none came to mind.

"Well," Zag said, "I suppose there's nothing for it but to look around. It can't be too far."

"She didn't build anything," Roc said.

"Her box was empty, Roc, you saw it. She built *something*."

As they searched, Zag repeated her trick—a strike of a plunger—on the various trees they passed. At the tenth tree, she said, "I think I hear something. This way, over here."

She led them to another clearing similar to the one they had started in. In its center was a vertical pipe, unsupported, with an open end pointed hopefully at the sky.

Roc couldn't stop laughing. For once, Seg didn't find the sound intolerably grating. When the Plumbess finally regained her composure, she said, "How's that for a source for you! If it rains for a couple days straight, a drop or two might find their way in. Ha! A shower that needs to be out in the pouring rain to work—a rain shower! You don't have to make those, girl, they happen on their own."

"Now, Roc," Zag replied, flustered. "Water *does* come from the sky. There's comprehension there, and that's progress. Progress. Eck, your shower should be a little more private, okay? People don't want to bathe out in the open like this. Now what's this here?"

To everyone's mutual surprise, Eck had taken the time to bury her own drain. Zag struck it with her plunger. "What did I tell you, Roc. More than just comprehension—this pipe's got a perfect pitch to it, and the girl didn't even have a level. What do you say to that?"

"Where does it go?" Roc asked, avoiding the question. "Let's get this farce over with and go home."

"Let's see," Zag said, and struck the pipe again. "It goes off this way."

It happened to be a very long pipe—they followed it, and every once in a while Zag would strike the ground to get further bearings. But then she suddenly stopped and motioned for everyone else to do the same. "Something's not right," she whispered. "All of you, stay here. Don't come any closer."

The stout Plumbess proceeded alone, disappearing into the dark foliage ahead. She returned just a few minutes later, and yet she looked years older. Her head shook lightly, like she'd lost motor control. She had a dazed look on her face and held her plunger limply to her side.

"What is it, Zag?" Roc asked, a touch of concern in her voice. "What's going on?"

"You don't want to know," Zag finally whispered, still looking lost. "Something like that shouldn't exist in these woods. Come . . . let's get back. Back to the Orphanage. Yes, come along. Eck, come here."

Their voices faded in the distance. Seg remained rooted in place, looking toward where the Plumbess had disappeared and reemerged. Although she trusted Zag that she didn't want to know, a morbid fascination held her there. She thought, for a moment, that she could feel something herself. Something out there, something terrible. What could Eck possibly have found? And why would she drain a shower to it?

"Girl!" Roc's voice cracked like a whip and brought her back to reality.

THE BALL

THE FOUNTAIN WAS the most impressive sight the Manor had to offer—after seeing it, Eck refused to be impressed by anything else. And Pipe Lord Marcus did try. He showed her tapestries woven out of pipes so thin that they were useless, and pipes that acted as mullions for stained-glass windows, and pipes that formed spiral staircases. They went through hallway after hallway until finally a door was announced as her own, a large oaken monstrosity covered in images of plungers.

"The room of the Plumbess," Pipe Lord Marcus said. "Very close to my own. It has one of the most luxurious baths in the Manor, dear Plumbess, as is befitting."

He turned to a servant from the contingent that followed them. "Would you mind showing her around, and how the bath works? And when she's done, show her to the west garden. I have some matters to attend to, but I'll meet her there."

"Of course, my lord."

Inside, the room felt like mildew, like considerable moisture had been trapped inside the walls for too long. A large canopy bed dominated the center, with each of its four posts in the shape of a plunger. She wondered—why did everything have to be shaped like a plunger, or made out of fake pipes? The bed didn't look like it would effectively unclog any toilets.

"I won't be wanting that," she told the servant. "Can you remove it from my room?"

"The bed, Plumbess? You'll want a smaller one, then? Less ostentatious?"

"No bed at all."

"What will you sleep on?"

"Does that matter to you?"

"I suppose not . . . " He trailed off into confusion.

Meanwhile, Eck had strolled over to the large window that comprised the western wall. It looked out over the Fountain, and she found herself again in awe.

The servant regained his footing. "Majestic sight, isn't it, Plumbess? The lifework of the previous Plumbess, rest her soul."

"I do like it," she said, but had already moved on. She was emptying out the contents of a nearby dresser. Not because she didn't like the contents, although she dumped them rather unceremoniously on the ground, but because the drawers seemed like the most appropriate place for her snakes. As she settled them in, the servant groaned but said nothing.

After that, she opened the doors of the large wardrobe and was overcome by a terrible mustiness. "And these," she said.

"Get rid of these. They aren't my clothes."

"They were the clothes of the previous Plumbess, Plumbess. She had a figure very similar to yours. I'm sure they'd fit quite—"

"I said they aren't my clothes."

"Yes, Plumbess."

From there she moved on to the bath Pipe Lord Marcus had mentioned, situated in an adjoining room. It was massive, made entirely of bronze and reminiscent of the Fountain. In imitation of Zag, she struck one of the pipes with her plunger and tilted her head to listen. Misunderstanding her intent, the servant gladly took it up as a subject of conversation.

"Finest-quality pipes, I assure you, in the finest of arrangements. A complete marvel of piping, if I may say. Designed and maintained by our very own group of elite engineers, who, if I may be so bold, are practically Plumbesses in their own right. *Plumbers*, if you will. Are . . . are you all right, Plumbess?"

She was in such a state of hilarity that her laughs came out more like convulsions. Eventually she managed to say, "*Plumbers*. That's wonderful."

He frowned. "Well, as I was saying. Right over here, there's one valve each for the five degrees of water. Coldest degree on the left, ascending precisely to the right. Just listen to me, explaining piping to a Plumbess! But it really is rather complicated. Here there are two valves for scented perfume—one mint, one a nice floral arrangement. This over here controls the mixing rate for a nice, even bath, and—Plumbess! What are you doing?"

She'd gotten her rubber boots off and was proceeding to her pants. "I'm taking a bath, aren't I? That's why you're explaining this to me?"

"But to just take off your clothes like that . . . "

"Is it designed to clean clothes as well?"

"No, no it isn't, but—"

When she then continued to take her pants off, the servant became so flustered that he left the room. It was all the same to her—she didn't need anyone explaining what the pipes did.

She started with the fifth degree of water and worked her way down. It was obvious by the third degree that the water was simply passed through a heat exchanger five times, once for each degree—she could feel the heat transfer coefficient expressing itself at every interval. When she'd configured it to the temperature she liked—she preferred a true fourth, and had to combine the bath's miscalculated third and fourth to get it—she turned to the perfumes.

The choice was obvious—she'd never heard of mint before—but seconds after turning the floral valve she was gagging uncontrollably. After gathering herself, she closed the valve and yelled at it, "These aren't flowers at all!" Then she drained the tub and started fresh.

An hour she bathed, an hour she floated there with her head submerged, listening as the drain slowly asserted itself on the contents of the tub—a sound that always calmed her. Then she got out, dried herself, and put on her Plumbess outfit so she could set out to find Pipe Lord Marcus. She didn't bother looking for the servant, deciding she could find her own way.

At the Orphanage she'd learned that Plumbing applied to buildings as well as pipes. A building flowed people. Every room, every hallway, had a discernible purpose. Five minutes alone in the Manor untaught her the same principle. So many of the hallways were dead legs, so many of the doors were valveless and impenetrable, so many of the rooms were stagnant pools of people. "What are you doing here?" she asked one such group. They didn't answer.

Yet she persevered, and was rewarded with Pipe Lord Marcus in one of the gardens. "I was expecting you earlier," he told her, looking at a contraption in his hands.

"What's that, sir?" she asked. Its glint had thoroughly caught her eye.

"Oh, this?" He smiled. "A small clock. It pumps water around in a circuit, and the inertia of the water discerns the time. A family heirloom."

"It's beautiful."

He nodded, slowly. "If you like this, let me show you the gardens. And you may call me Marcus, by the way. No need for . . . for 'sir' from a Plumbess such as yourself."

Just then, the servant from before rounded a corner, a look of disdain on his face. "I tried to find her, my lord, but she wasn't in her room."

"It's all right, she's here now. Come along."

They stepped through a pair of doors and were confronted by trees inside a building. There was the taste of nature—dirt, grass, fertile smells—but there were also walls, and a crystal ceiling, and so much piping running through it all. Eck preferred nature itself, not some perversion. But still she liked it better than the room of the Plumbess, which she was quick to voice.

"Can this be my room instead?" she asked, looking up at an impressive poplar that spanned tens of meters into the air.

Marcus laughed as if it were a joke. Then he looked at her

and saw the sincerity in her eyes. "It's not a very private place, dear Plumbess. Anyone could just walk in here at any time of day."

"I won't bother them," Eck promised. "If I slept under that bush right there, no one would notice me."

"Under a bush? That's hardly suitable for a Plumbess. You'll sleep on a bed—"

The servant discreetly shook his head.

Marcus changed course. "Who am I to deny you, dear Plumbess? But not this garden. There's a different one, with less thoroughfare. That one would be more preferable for us both."

The servant raised an eyebrow. To him, Marcus said, "The north garden—see that it's done. And see that it's made *private*."

"Yes, my lord." The servant departed.

Marcus then guided her through the sprawling garden, extolling its wealth and beauty. More than once Eck corrected him with respect to both Plumbing and planting, but he shrugged off every correction with an "if you say so, dear Plumbess." He had a much firmer grip on the resources that were required, the personnel and the money, and Eck was equally less disposed to correct him.

He showed her isolated idylls, mechanical hills, ponds in alcoves, terraces formed by piping. He showed her rows of fruits and vegetables shelved like books and talked about agricultural output and the dietary needs of the average peasant. She tried smiling at all the right times to show that she appreciated the attention. And overall, he seemed rather agreeable himself, if Eck was anyone to judge.

He stopped in front of a stone statue set next to a miniature fountain whose bowl was so full it disrupted the flow. The statue was of a man with a heavy brow and a hawk-like gaze. His stone shirt resembled Marcus's own, washed of colors.

"This is my late father," Marcus told her, and himself showed due reverence to the past royalty.

"Is he . . . " She hesitated, but then continued. "Is he inside of the statue?"

Marcus stared at her. "No, no he isn't. We have a graveyard for that sort of thing."

"A graveyard?"

"A place where we bury dead people. Isn't there something like that at the Orphanage?"

"No," she replied. People rarely died at the Orphanage, but in the rare instance, the body was burned on a funeral pyre. "Buried bodies . . . the hole would have to be rather large for a body, wouldn't it? Aren't you afraid of rupturing pipes?"

"There are no pipes running through the graveyard, fortunately."

"Oh."

The Pipe Lord looked at his small clock again. This time, Eck thought she could hear the water flowing through it. It had a strange cadence. Was that what time sounded like?

"Well, Plumbess," he said, "court convenes twice a day, once at second bell and once at seventh. The seventh bell is about to ring. I'd like to announce your appointment, and I'd like you to be there with me. Is this acceptable?"

"Yes," she said.

"Let's be off, then."

The Pipe Lord struck off at a very different pace than the

one they'd used through the garden. As they emerged into the hallways and chambers, Eck discovered that some of the doors she'd assumed were valveless were what he called *locked*, and that only he and a few select servants had the capacity to open them. It made a certain amount of sense to Eck—if she, a Plumbess, could have certain unique capabilities for Plumbing, then he, a Pipe Lord, could have certain unique capabilities for buildings. The two, as she now understood, were very distinct fields.

She heard the throne room before she entered it. There were voices—so many that none of them were distinct. The seventh bell reverberated around them like a river of water filling a subterranean channel. They walked between two large doors and a wondrous sight greeted them.

There were more people than Eck had ever seen in one place—there were never more than ten or so Plumbesses at the Orphanage, and the orphans themselves didn't take up much space. On the far shore of the crowd was the throne, a massive thing made of welded gold pipes. To her distaste, Eck noticed that it too served no utility. Another thing she'd eventually have to fix. Behind the throne was an enormous panel of windows that looked out onto the Fountain just outside.

Marcus sat in his throne, his back to the Fountain. Apparently the view wasn't for him. As was customary, Eck stood to his left. She clasped her hands in front of her and waited. As the last tones of the seventh bell faded, so too did the noise of the crowd.

Marcus began to speak, with a voice that somehow filled the expansive room. "Barons and baronesses. It is a pleasure to see you all again. Before we begin with the evening's scheduled activities, I would like to make a few announcements, although I'm sure the rumors have had sufficient time to diffuse through the Manor. This morning it was my pleasure to discover that the Manor had a leak. It was brought to my attention by a motherless child who recommended a certain Plumbess residing in Storm's End. I Called that Plumbess, and now she stands by my side. Please, welcome to the Manor of Storms—Plumbess Eck. May she continue where Plumbess Sol left off, and lead us to further prosperity."

It was a polite cheer that followed, but it was still deafening to Eck. She modestly cast her glance downward and bared her teeth in the imitation of a smile. Soon, the noise passed and Marcus spoke again. "To commemorate the occasion—in the place of tomorrow's second court and all the time after it, until sleep overtakes the last of us—there will be a ball in honor of the old Plumbess and the new. What better way to express our joy? Be sure to spread the word that all persons of noble piping are invited and encouraged to attend."

Instead of a cheer, this announcement was greeted by murmurs.

"And now, let us return to the court at hand. Baron Scoll, I believe you have a speech prepared for us?"

"I do, your lordship," said a portly man in stately pipes.

An hour dragged by, an hour of Eck standing and giving the pretense of rapt attention. On the inside, she was still frightened by the noise of the affair. But then the eighth bell toned and the court dissolved under formalities similar to how it began.

Marcus turned to her. "It feels wonderful to have a Plumbess by my side again at court. I feel more confident, if you can forgive a man his puerile fancies. But still, it's good to have you, Eck. About tomorrow—I want you to have a new dress for the occasion. One just to your liking. The royal tailor will see to it in the morning. Will that be suitable?"

"Okay," she said, but with a hint of doubt that only grew as she stepped into the tailor's atelier next morning. Mannequins littered the floor and walls, surrounded by long, tangled threads, jagged sets of shears, and strange machines. The tailor himself was a small man with hardly any hair.

"A dress," he said. "For a ball. I know all about it, yes, Ms. Plumbess. I've taken the liberty of selecting a few popular styles for you, to help with your choice." He showed her to a gathering of mannequins arranged like they were having a flippant conversation in the room's disheveled corner. They looked an eerie amount like real baronesses.

She was surprised to discover what a dress entailed. "I don't think I could unclog a toilet wearing one of these," she told the tailor.

"And no one would ask you to," he replied.

"If I have to pick one, then this," she said. Her choice was mainly based on the mannequin being taller than the others.

"And do you know what cloth you would like?"

She'd never once considered that there was more than one kind of cloth. She expressed her ignorance and he proceeded to show her an absurd selection of fabrics that he randomly designated as cotton, silk, velvet, or wool in a similarly confounding number of weaves and colors. Eventually she settled on a blue fabric that he called flax. She picked it because the texture looked a lot like the skin of a snake.

Then he insisted on measuring her, even though she gave

him her exact measurements: her arms were nearly the size of a standard household waterline, her waist the size of a sewer main. Still, he insisted, and in the end had his way—pulling on her arms, legs, and waist in all directions until he was finally satisfied.

"I'll have it done before this evening," he told the servant who accompanied her. "A tight timeline, but I can manage."

The servant then escorted her back to her room, which was now a garden. A bare minimum of furniture had been placed in between the various bushes and trees—among them, the dresser from before. Her snakes, though, were no longer housed in its drawers. She'd insisted they wander the garden freely. The servant eyed the one he could see with mistrust—a python, looking down at them from a nearby tree.

"Don't like snakes?" she asked him, a sly smile on her face.

"I don't like anything dangerous," he replied.

"Then you don't like people," she said, "and this place is full of those. They're much worse than snakes. I can prove it to you. Come here, Shash." She extended her arms up toward the tree, and in response the snake unwound from its branch and lowered its weight down into her arms. When she turned around to present him to the servant, the servant was already gone.

The dress arrived several hours later, and she tried it on in the lonely solace of her garden. For a mirror she used the glimmering façade of a small waterfall, which portrayed her accurately enough. What she saw wasn't a Plumbess. Her arms and shoulders were bare, with a mere flap of cloth looped around her upper arm on both sides. The shoes that supposedly went with the dress left her calves exposed, which seemed to her a safety hazard. She didn't have her plunger either—Marcus requested she leave it behind for the ball, which left her feeling even more exposed than the dress did.

She was fairly certain that a Plumbess was never supposed to take off her black-and-white outfit. And yet she'd seen the extensive wardrobe of the last Plumbess and furthermore doubted that Marcus would recommend it if it wasn't allowed. Still, it was discomforting to look at her reflection and not see a Plumbess. She did see, however, the outlines of a snake, which was perhaps the only reason she was able to gather her courage and leave her garden just in time for the seventh bell.

"Ah, Plumbess," a servant said as she exited her garden. "Right this way."

"I can find my own way," she replied.

"I'm sure you could. Follow me."

She grudgingly accepted, which was probably for the best as they took some unexpected turns, winding up a few floors to the higher reaches of the Manor. But soon there was a sound, growing with every intersection, that clearly marked the path.

"What is that?" she asked.

"A pipe organ," he said.

They entered the ballroom, and it was filled with even more people than the Pipe Lord's court. Its center was dominated by the pipe organ, an absurd combination of a thousand pipes, all with different diameters, ascending into the broad open space of the vaulted ceiling. She could see a man seated at its operator interface, reading from a set of instructions as he opened and closed valves. The result was a pulsing music, so strange and yet so vaguely familiar. For a moment she strained her brain to better sift her memory, but gave up after getting no results.

The barons and baronesses were dressed up in what must have been their fineries. The men looked like misplaced tubing, all angular and stiff. The women looked like exotic birds that had no business being so close to such machinery. The servant tried leading her in, but Eck resisted near the doorway, where there was still a little room to breathe.

Then Marcus spoke, cutting through the noise as he always did. He stood on a dais overlooking the crowd. He wore a black suit, less ostentatious than the barons and yet somehow just as regal. He cleared his throat just once and the pipe organ itself stopped to listen, although its deeper notes took longer to fade into silence.

"Just a few words, and then the pleasantries may begin. I wanted to make clear one last time the reason for the occasion, and she has just arrived—Plumbess Eck."

Everyone turned to look at her, and Eck wilted under the collective gaze.

"Tonight is for her, although I will allow and insist that everyone enjoy themselves. Be sure to eat our fine selection of food and drink, piped in fresh from the kitchens"—he gestured broadly to his left—"and engage in a fair amount of dancing. But first, of course, the dance between the Pipe Lord and his Plumbess."

The space around Eck immediately cleared. The pipe organ wound up again into a brisk, cyclical array of sounds. Marcus descended from the dais and walked to her. He extended his hand—his left hand. She hesitated, but took it.

He physically took her over, lifting her and pushing her in a rhythm that complemented the pipe organ's. Her dress spun out around her, scales shining in the light of a thousand candles. The crowd of barons and baronesses around them simply watched.

After Marcus had taken her around a complete circuit, he said, "You dance fairly well, Plumbess."

She had yet to move anything of her own accord, except initially taking his hand. "Oh," she said.

Eventually the song guttered out, but the pipe organ pulsed back into motion with slightly different tones and rhythms. This time everyone joined in with the dancing, large men everywhere dragging birdlike women, all in a way that seemed exceedingly dangerous to Eck.

She had to lean very close to Marcus to make herself heard. "There are drinks in here?" she asked. She felt, suddenly, very thirsty.

"Right over there." He pointed to pipes that she could now clearly see, surrounded by a congregation of people. "There's a bureaucratic matter I have to resolve first, but I'll join you there very soon."

They parted. She pushed her way through the frenzy until she finally arrived at the people accessing the drinks. One man in particular seemed to be blocking the flow, his eyes looking down expectantly at Eck. By way of conversation, she said, "What's your favorite pipe?"

"My favorite pipe? Why should I have a favorite pipe?"

"You're a Pipe Baron, right? It stands to reason."

He hmphed at her and turned his shoulders, allowing her to slip through. Then there was a lady, a baroness in pale green lined with cream-colored down. To her she said, "You're not actually a bird, right?"

"I beg your pardon?"

"It's a yes or no question. Are you actually a bird?"

"No, I'm not."

"Oh good, that's a relief."

That conversation also didn't last long. Eck found herself instead at a pipe, which she felt much more comfortable with. She took a nearby glass and opened a valve to fill it. The liquid that came out was dark red, which was very much outside her expectations. She tasted it anyway, and immediately regretted her decision.

"What's wrong with this water!?" she yelled at another baron, who shrugged as if innocent.

Another baron walked up to her, looking lost. He slurred, "Plumbess . . . Plumbess." Then, without further prelude, he put his hand on her bare shoulder.

Physical contact was difficult enough for her when she consented and was prepared, as with Marcus during the dance and, to a lesser degree, the tailor measuring her. But the sheer surprise of the way the baron touched her caused her to fall back on a primal instinct—she hissed at him, which drew more than a few amazed stares.

A voice arrived to save her—the voice of Marcus. "Baron Marlow, if you could please give the Plumbess a little bit more room. She's still acclimating to our strange ways. There you go, that's a good baron."

"I was just . . . " the baron replied, struggling with his feet. "Congratulations. New Wombess, very happy."

"A nice sentiment. And now that you've expressed it, if you could give me and the *Plumbess* some time alone."

The baron nodded, the paragon of understanding, and then shuffled off. Marcus took his vacated spot. "Balls. Always the same," he said, laughing. And then, getting a better look at her, "I apologize, Plumbess. Are you all right?"

"I just need space," she said.

"Well, there's a balcony there on the other side of the room. Probably not too many people out there, not when there's dancing to be had. There's someone else I should talk to, but I'll meet you there presently." He walked away.

Once again, Eck struggled through throngs of people who resembled her in no way. A pair of dancers bumped into her, to which she responded, "Who taught you how to dance?" But the music took them away before the question even registered.

She went very near another set of pipes that apparently conveyed food. There seemed to be a problem, though: an unstoppable outflow was leaching food out onto the dance floor. Barons and baronesses tried barricading with their hands, or plates, or their sheer girth, but that only incapacitated them for further action. Servants surrounded, vying to lend help where they could but contributing, in general, very little.

Eck's concerns were elsewhere. She emerged onto the balcony and was immediately relieved by the change of atmosphere. A cool breeze came from the world, carrying the smell of trees with it. Somewhere below her, invisible in the darkness, was the implacable Fountain. She looked to where it might be.

She was finally starting to breathe better when the door opened and closed behind her, letting out for a moment a screeching of people and a new pipe organ configuration to accompany it. She expected Marcus, and was already smiling when she saw that it was the baron from before. The one who had touched her.

"Womplumb," he managed. "I forgive you, for whatever back there. I hope you accept your apology." He took wavering steps toward her. She stepped back, back toward the Fountain, until her back touched the balustrade and she wouldn't go any farther. He put his hand out again, like before. Like he would touch her.

If she'd had her plunger, she would've killed him then and there—there was no doubt in her mind. As it was, she felt essentially defenseless. Still, she wouldn't give up without a fight. In the moment before he touched her, she reached out a mental hand and grabbed at his head.

She found, to her surprise, a pipe. One that she knew, on a visceral level, to be meant for waste. It was slimy to the touch, constricted, bloated. Without really knowing what she did, she connected it above, to the man's source, making a circle that was contrary to all Plumbing.

The result was immediate. The baron began violently twitching and foaming at the mouth. As the door to the ballroom opened again, he was slowly slumping to the ground, which unfortunately dragged his body across Eck's legs and exposed feet.

"Eck?" a voice asked. It was Marcus. "Is that . . . is that Baron Marlow? What did you do to him?"

"I don't know," she replied, which was the truth. She must have looked shaken, because he took her by the hand and supported her as they returned to the ballroom. On their way in they passed servants hauling buckets of food, presumably from the overflowing pipe.

"Would one of you help the estimable baron to his feet and see that he makes it comfortably to his bed?" Marcus said, pointing at the human pile they left behind.

One of the servants detached himself and tended to the baron. The rest inconspicuously emptied their buckets over the balustrade and into the darkness below.

WATER RIGHTS

AS THE CARRIAGE trundled through the desolate city of Hope Springs, Pipe Lord Carral quickly misremembered what they were doing. Perhaps it was the Plumbess's grave that had taken him to a different time entirely. "Young lady," he said to Seg in a confidential whisper. "I'm on my way to answer a Service Call. A Plumbess Mar, if I remember correctly. Highly recommended. What do you think I should say? I've never been good at the formalities."

Seg was disposed to just go along with it. "Tell her the truth—that you'll appreciate her services. A Plumbess would like to hear that. And don't forget a pen and paper, to draw up a Contract of Work. Plumbesses are rather bureaucratic, from what I've heard."

The Pipe Lord patted his lapels, perhaps looking for a pen, but naturally found nothing there. "I will appreciate her, that's certain. I expect a lot of good things from her."

"And I'm sure she'll live up to them," Seg said, but there was a hollowness to her reassurance. She was looking out the window at dry ponds and motionless fountains, at outhouses—*outhouses*—right in the middle of a city. Not even Plumbing at all, the refrain repeated in her mind.

How could a good Plumbess have left a town in such a state? Could the intervening forty years really have taken away so much? How long until Seg's own contributions became wasted away and forgotten, relics living only in the mind of a senile man?

The carriage finally collapsed to a stop in front of a hovel. Although in no better state than any of those around it, Seg soon recognized it as the Pipe Lord's home. A single golden pipe stood at its top, nearly vertical but loose at a few of its joints.

A man was waiting for them. He set the carriage's stairs, opened its door, and helped the Pipe Lord out, all with far more grace than the liveryman himself would have managed. When the man returned to shut the carriage back up, he seemed surprised to find Seg inside.

"Oh," he said. "Are you all right, ma'am?"

He was looking at the dried blood and abraded skin of her neck—the jolting ride had reopened her wound.

"I'm fine. It's just this necklace. My Lead."

"You should probably take it off if it's causing that much trouble."

"I can't. It marks me as a Plumbess."

"A . . . Plumbess, you say? I . . . when my father said he was off to get a Plumbess, I didn't believe him. He's done that before—ridden the carriage out to retrieve some mirage of a memory, and of course he always comes back empty-handed. There's no stopping him when he's like that, so today I just wished him luck. And it's a good thing I did, because what a wonderful mirage you turned out to be—a little pale, but seemingly real. Are you still transitioning into the material world, a ghost of some sort?"

He extended a hand to assist her out, and gave a sly smile.

Seg blushed heavily due to the mention of her paleness and extended her own hand. "If this is reality, then the mirage I came from is in a much better state. I've never seen a place so ruined."

"Just arrived and you're already insulting our town?"

"If it deserves it, yes."

He laughed. "You'll find that it does, yes. This town has everything it deserves, nothing more. But where are my manners—my name is Gregor, or Baron Gregor if you must. Son of the Pipe Lord, if you haven't guessed."

He gave another smile, but it was less convincing than the last. His entire nature had a desiccated feel to it—even his hair seemed dry, like nature had intended it brown but the world had left it sandy blond. His nose suffered from further failings, and yet he maintained a regal bearing.

"Plumbess Seg," she responded. "Pleasure to meet you."

"Would someone open this door?" Carral called from the porch of his hovel. He didn't wait for a response—with a strange strength he pried the seemingly stiff hinges into motion. The door swung open so hard that the whole house shook. He then turned back to look at Gregor and Seg. "There's the Plumbess's room right in here. A servant will prepare it for Plumbess Mar, yes."

"There's not a room, actually," Gregor said to Seg. "It collapsed a few years ago, nothing left of it. No, you'll have to stay somewhere else, unless you want to share a room with me. I do believe the Peregrin household, right across the street, would be both vacant and suitable."

The passing casual suggestion of sharing a room shook Seg, but she chose to ignore it. "A vacant place would be nice. And I'd be just as interested in some food and water—it's been a long journey. If someone could show me the house and bring some food there."

"Nonsense!" Gregor exclaimed, strangely reproducing his father's exuberant outbursts. "There will be a feast tonight with all the barons. We'll be discussing the trial there, and your presence would be perfect."

As much as Seg wanted some time to rest on her own, the mention of a trial caught her curiosity.

In short time, she was seated at a small, round wooden table. Pipe Lord Carral sat immediately to her right, Gregor to her left. Six other barons were with them, and the eight were packed rather tightly.

Gregor was the only baron under sixty or so—the others had impressive grey mustaches and suits that frayed unbelievably at the seams.

The Pipe Lord led them in a rambling grace before the food was served. "Barons," he said. "Peasants. Food is nothing but what is eaten. If the sky . . . if a river—do we have the river?"

"No, not yet," Gregor contributed.

"May the rivers flow our way, then. Because . . . fish are good. The largest fish I ever caught was six stones. The weight was six stones, mind you, not the fish. I don't know why we weigh food with rocks, it doesn't seem sanitary. Bless this food . . . this manna from the desert. It's a miracle that food could be produced in the desert, but here it is. Thanks, gods. And let us pray that it isn't leavened, because if it is there will be trouble. A pipe that doesn't—"

"Amen," Gregor said, and the other barons grumbled their agreement.

They seemed like a polite group of people. A lot of muttered niceties—an "if I may" and a "pardon" or two—accompanied the general clatter as food was distributed. A particularly ancient man took it upon himself to serve the Plumbess her plate.

One thing from Carral's grace seemed distressingly true—the food looked like it came directly from the desert. The carrots were so gnarled that even boiled they looked raw. They were accompanied by some other tubers that Seg didn't recognize and a plate of something that looked suspiciously like sticks. Seg was accustomed to the colorful produce of the Orphanage, and even in her hunger she only hesitantly ate.

"You arrived just in time," Gregor told her before eating anything himself. "Tomorrow the trial begins in earnest, and we could use the help of a Plumbess. The town against Baron Seth."

Seg looked around at the old men seated there.

"He's not here, of course. He prefers to dine elsewhere," Gregor explained.

"He's got a whole river. A river!" one of the other barons exclaimed, so indignant that he fell into a fit of phlegmy wheezing.

If there was a river in the town, Seg hadn't seen it. It must have been small.

"All to himself," another baron complained. "Does he even use it? Has anyone seen him use it?"

"We'll use it," Gregor said, nodding and chewing a few carrots. "With the Law itself at our side, we'll take it from him. If we don't, you might not have much to do, Plumbess. That river is the only running water in town."

"There's still the Pipe Lord's Well," Carral said.

"I said *running* water, father. The Well doesn't run."

"It used to," the old Pipe Lord countered, pouting like a child.

"And I'm sure those were lovely days, but they're gone now. Perhaps, though—perhaps the Plumbess can bring them back."

All conversation, all chewing, stopped as everyone present turned to Seg. She set down the carrot she'd been contemplating. "I'd . . . like to see this river first, before making any promises."

"There's a fence around it," a baron explained.

"She might be able to see over the fence."

"Or, hmph, or there's the hole over on Bradburry's Hill, if it hasn't been patched up yet. You can see the river through the, hmph, hole."

"I've been meaning to have that hole fixed. I've got a boy, he could probably fix that hole up right good."

"We will not," Gregor said firmly, "fix a fence that shouldn't exist. And are we here to discuss business, or aren't we?"

That brought the barons back to their senses—they all seemed ready to discuss business. Carral especially, who held his fork in his mottled hand and stabbed it forward with firm resolve.

Gregor continued. "Now, I don't have to tell you that tomorrow is important. How we start will very much influence how we end, and the course of everything in between. That old miser Seth will clamp down hard on his 'possession' and bark at anyone that comes near it, but if we present a unified front, if we hit him with the unbiased hammer of the Law itself, he'll crumple into dust."

Men nodded.

"So, Baron Ronald, if you could have one last talk with the judge to make sure he hasn't gotten cold feet. And Baron Martin, make sure to bring your knife. If worse comes to worst—"

"The Pipe Lord's Hose!" Carral interjected, standing up in his sudden agitation. "We must bring the Pipe Lord's Hose, mustn't we?"

"Yes, father," Gregor said, pushing the old man back down into his chair. "Of course."

The rest of the evening was spent on other trivial details pertinent to the trial ahead. Afterward, Gregor himself escorted Seg to the vacant house across the street.

"Thank you," she said, standing in the dilapidated entryway.

"It's not much," he replied. "There's no bath, for instance. If you want one of those, you'll have to petition the Pipe Lord for an appointment in the Pipe Lord's bath, and then you'll have to wait to see if he grants your request."

Seg frowned.

"Just kidding," he said, smiling again. "That's what the peasants have to do. You're a Plumbess. Just ask my father and I'm sure he'll let you take anyone's slot. Or, on an even more hopeful note—if one is allowed hope in this town—perhaps tomorrow we'll have a river, and we won't have to talk about bath appointments anymore. That's the kind of world I'd like to live in."

He left, and Seg was exhausted enough from travelling to give herself directly into sleep.

In the morning she had a paltry breakfast with the barons and listened as they ironed over their plans one last time. Then she set off on her own course, which led her first to Hope Spring's valve house.

The valve house was little more than a shack, and in fact was missing one of its walls. The exposed side faced several wooden posts set in one-meter intervals. When she entered, she asked the surly man she found there, "What happened here?"

"What, the wall? They took it out for an expansion, I think. For more valves. But the last thing we really need is more valves. A work in progress, I suppose."

"And how long has it been in progress?"

"As long as I've been here."

Seg surveyed the room, if it could be called one. It was an impressive disaster. "Do you have a pipegram, at least?" she asked, not seeing one. "I thought all Pipe Lords were required to have one."

"Right over here," he said, getting lazily to his feet. He walked to one of the two fully formed corners of the room and pulled a tarp off of a table. Underneath was a machine attached to a real pipe—one that put to shame all the half-formed pipes around it. The pipe went straight to the Orphanage, and shared its grandeur.

"I'd like to send a message to the Orphanage," she said.

"Okay, hold on there." He opened some nearby valves and flipped a lever or two. Then he stationed himself in front of a valve block where each of the valves had a letter on it. He pressed a few of them, and every time he did the machine created a sound that it sent down the pipe. A few moments later, sounds returned. A clever bit of machinery turned their vibrations into written words, and a nearby readout said, "The Orphanage listens."

"There we go. Now what do you want to tell those witches?"

"I'm a Plumbess too, you idiot. Move over."

"Hey, wait a minute, I'm perfectly qualified—"

Although the man was much larger than her, she had a plunger. She pointed it threateningly at his stomach. "If you don't move, I'll destroy you. I'll shorten your digestive tract to a single centimeter in length, and you won't be able to put food in without it already being out. Now are you going to move or not?"

The man vacated the valve house entirely, and Seg took his place at the valve block. "Seg here," she typed.

"Hold on," came the reply. She almost felt like she could understand the sounds the pipe made, but she looked at the readout anyway.

Several minutes passed, during which she wiped the dust from the pipegram. When the machine finally clanged back into motion, she nearly lost her hand for the small sake of cleanliness.

The readout said, "Roc here."

Even though they parted on poor terms, Seg was glad to

hear from the Plumbess after so much travelling alone. "How is the Orphanage?" she typed.

"Almost its old self," Roc replied.

"I am now the Hope Springs Plumbess," she then typed, feeling a small pride despite everything.

A hesitation entered the conversation, transmitted over so much distance. Then Roc said, "Congratulations, Seg. Have you seen Eck?"

Seg nearly left the valve house, question unanswered. Somehow Eck continued to interpose herself between all of Seg's achievements.

"No, I haven't," she typed after settling herself.

"I've asked every Pipe Lord, but none have seen her."

"If she went anywhere, it was to that Marcus. You suggested it to her yourself."

"I tried there first, but they say they haven't seen her."

"I have my own problems. It's very dry here," Seg replied. "Nothing works."

"Then fix it," Roc said.

As Seg left the valve house, those three words weighed heavily on her soul. It all seemed too far gone to fix, confirmed by a tour she made of the town. A closer look at the ponds showed why they were dry: the irrigation channels that led away from them had been hacked into by further irrigation channels, which were themselves hacked into by makeshift pipework, like a leech bleeding a leech bleeding a vacuum.

She took a look through the hole in the fence on Bradburry's Hill, and wasn't encouraged by what she saw. It was a stream at best. Not believing that a town could be so dry, she Plumbed the ground, which led her to a well close to the Pipe

Lord's hovel. She stared down into its abyss—the groundwater was so low that she couldn't even see its surface. But she could smell a slight humidity in its air, and it was the closest thing to hope that she'd found yet. A strange, narrow hose was piped along the well's side. The Pipe Lord's Well and Hose, she assumed. Unimpressed, she moved on.

It was midday, and she was studying the exposed roots of an ancient cedar when she noticed a gathering stream of people. Since it was the most convincing stream she'd seen in weeks, she joined it. There were bent old women and toothless men, all with strangely vacant looks in their eyes. They didn't seem to notice her. They brought her, as she suspected, to the courthouse, where she took a seat in the back.

At the front of the room she saw Gregor, in quiet consultation with the judge. To their side was a bench full of barons, one of whom she'd never seen before—that would be Baron Seth. He had an imperious wig, and was frowning so hard that his chin was invisible. The barons and the judge were separated from the expectant crowd of peasants by a small but well-observed open space.

Eventually the conversation between Gregor and the judge ended, and the judge declared to all, "Let's get this session started then, shall we? The town against Baron Seth on the matter of the Hope Springs River. We'll start with some opening remarks by the prosecution, represented by our own Baron Gregor."

"Thank you," Gregor told the judge. "Thank you." He began pacing back and forth in the open space between judge and audience, with an occasional glance at the bench of barons for moral support.

"Hope Springs," he said, "surely got its name from some-where. Allow me to speculate—it's because we used to be a beacon of hope, to other cities and to humanity as a whole, at some long-forgotten time in the past. What changed, you ask? What could've gone so wrong that we'd end up here, as we are? I have an answer. Some greedy, clutching man, some pro-genitor of this despicable Baron Seth—"

"See here!" Baron Seth cried in a frog-like voice, but he was quickly silenced by both the judge and virulent booing from the audience.

Gregor embraced the interruption. "That the man can't even observe proper court etiquette is very telling—but yes, some greedy, clutching man has put his talons around the throat of our town, its lifeblood, its river, and choked the hope right out of it. Have you ever *seen* the hope choked out of something?" the baron asked, flourishing. "Well, at the very least you've seen the aftermath. This place is a husk, this place is a carcass. But it doesn't have to be like this. With that river, which belongs to the town and the Pipe Lord *by right*, we could be reborn. We could fill up some of those old pipes we've got buried everywhere, and our town name could make sense again. It's possible that some of us could even bathe more—"

His last statement drew so much applause from the au-dience that, rather than continuing his speech as he seemed ready to do, he just sat down and ended on the unexpected high note.

The judge said, "And now, I suppose, we'll hear a word from the defendant, Baron Seth."

Instead of standing in front of the judge as Gregor had done, Baron Seth chose not to move from where he sat, apparently preferring to deliver his wrath obscured as he was in the corner. "This *Baron* Gregor," he declaimed, "will one day own the lands of his father, Pipe Lord Carral, when that old man finally dies like he's been promising to do. This Baron *Gregor* believes in property rights for *his* property, but what about *my* property? My father owned the river, and his father before him, and so on and so on, in perpetuity. By right I hold that land, and those waters—"

"But he uses none of them, while the city dries to death," Gregor interrupted. "No, instead he lets his river drift off into the desert, where it does nothing but feed the cactuses."

"At least the cactuses have upstanding moral character, unlike anyone here!"

"If the town can make better use of it—"

"Riparian!" Baron Seth cried over the rising din. "Riparian!"

"That's enough," the judge told the angered baron. "If the prosecution would like to call its first witness?"

"Yes, I would," Gregor said. "She arrived just yesterday, the newest addition to our dying city—I call upon Plumbess Seg."

The din got even louder. Seg could hear as the children around her, and even quite a few adults, asked what a Plumbess was. She was interested to hear someone's response, but was interrupted by a firm strike of the judge's gavel, which mostly silenced the room. Curious about the gavel's effect, she tried then and there to imitate the sound of its authority, but with her plunger. The bench she struck disintegrated under the force. "Sorry," she told the people who had been sitting there, and strode to the front of the room to take a seat next to the judge.

"Now, Plumbess," Gregor said, looking briefly at her as he began to pace again. "In your professional opinion, what would you say a river is for?"

"First and foremost," Seg replied, "I think you should be honest about what you have, so that you're not disappointed by the results I can give you. What is behind that fence is not a river. It's a stream at best."

Another commotion broke out. No one seemed more upset than Baron Seth himself, who lost his wig.

"But," she continued, "to answer your question, a river can be for anything. When there's a dying town, though, and people very much in need, I would say that there's a moral obligation by the people who have the authority to see that the river is put to good use."

"And can you do that, Plumbess? Can you put it to good use?"

"I have some ideas," Seg said. "Some small projects that would show immediate improvement around here, yes."

Gregor, looking content, rested his case. The judge, in collusive sympathy, tried to call a recess, but the audience had become so unruly that even with his gavel he couldn't silence them. Seg tried again, on a sturdier wall, and plunged the room into silence. After that, recess came easily.

The non-Seth barons convened, and Seg joined them. "Very good," Gregor was telling them. "About as good a beginning as we could hope for. A Plumbess, right out of the gate. Yes, good."

"The Hose!" Carral exclaimed, excited again. "Let them see our generosity."

"Yes, father. We'll have it brought. Damien?"

The liveryman from the day before scrambled out of the courthouse to fetch it.

"The Plumbess, she'll carry it," Carral continued, insistent through a haze of incomprehension.

"Carry . . . the Hose?" Seg asked, confused.

"To water the peasants," Gregor clarified.

"I'd rather not," Seg said.

"One thing!" Carral cried. "I ask for one thing, as a Pipe Lord to his Plumbess! Shouldn't . . . ! Haven't . . . !? Didn't . . . ?"

"Fine," she said.

A few moments later the liveryman returned, carrying the tattered Hose. It was leaking in numerous places, a flimsy valve on its end. Through the window of the courthouse Seg could see where the Hose wound off toward the Pipe Lord's Well.

The liveryman kneeled in front of the Pipe Lord and presented the Hose as if it were some kind of sacred sword.

"Not me," Carral told him. "The Plumbess."

Seg walked over and took the Hose from his extended arms.

It was about as strange as she expected. She walked up to the benches of peasants, and they held out cupped hands longingly. She watered each in turn. She was surprised to find even the barons holding out cupped hands, and she watered them as well.

She made the mistake, though, of stopping in front of Baron Seth.

"Get that Hose out of my face, Plumbess. Gloating around with it like it's some kind of royal blessing. Get it out of my face before I do something drastic."

The next day, the hole in the fence on Bradburry's Hill was fixed. It was a declaration of war, although no one was quite sure who made it.

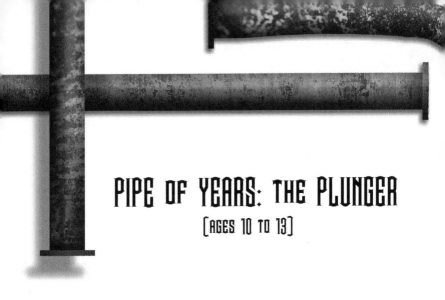

PIPE OF YEARS: THE PLUNGER
[AGES 10 TO 13]

EVERY PLUMBESS USED her plunger in a distinctive way. They all shared Plumbing as a foundation—they all unclogged drains, opened valves, healed people, and birthed babies. But the similarities seemed to end there. Even the way they *held* it was different—Seg had watched every Plumbess in the Orphanage unclog at least one drain, and it ranged from Plumbess Tes, who practically dunked her hand in with every pulse, to Plumbess Roc, who held on to the very tip of the handle like she was after all the leverage she could get.

Oftentimes the most distinctive of uses didn't even look like Plumbing. There was a Plumbess, Plumbess Ark, who cooked with hers on holidays. Seg technically wasn't allowed in the kitchens, but still she'd seen the domineering Plumbess mixing batters, probing temperatures, and keeping the staff in line with her plunger. It left a vivid impression on Seg.

Zag would find things with hers. All Plumbesses knew how to dowse for water, but Zag perfected and extended the art. She used it to find buried piping, or lost possessions, or—distressingly—apprentices avoiding their duties. On days when Seg knew she couldn't deal with Roc, she would hide in some garden alcove or storage closet, but before long she'd hear the resounding thud of a plunger on the ground—she could *feel* the pulse of sound seek her out—and seconds later, she'd be discovered. The only person who seemed able to avoid Zag's technique was her own apprentice, Eck, who could sometimes disappear for days and leave her mentor at wit's end.

Roc, meanwhile, seemed to perfect the art of striking a child. Whenever she thought Seg was disobeying or not listening, or even just in danger of not listening, she'd give her a sharp rap that would sting for hours. One day, Seg saw her mentor use what she swore was the same strike—a sharp turn of the wrist with the plunger grasped at the very tip of the handle—to fix a pipe that looked beyond repair. Seg was immediately filled with indignation, and empathy, for the pipe.

"Is that what you've been hitting me with? Some pipe-fixing maneuver?" Seg complained.

Roc's response was to use it again, on Seg, which of course stopped her from further complaining.

Even with Roc's aversive example, Seg developed a thorough reverence of the plunger. According to the Plumbesses, plungers were dangerous to use, and therefore not given to apprentices until they'd demonstrated their maturity, but that didn't stop Seg from fantasizing. She spent hours daydreaming about how she would use hers. Naturally, she gravitated toward Zag's technique. She would have Eck bury something, and then, using a stick, broom, or whatever came to hand, she would strike the ground and listen.

The results were never promising—a fact that Eck would

cheerily remind her of. Although the snake wouldn't attempt to use a stick like Seg, she would always watch and offer useless criticism.

"That's not a plunger, that's a stick."

"I know, Eck."

"Then why are you trying to use it like a plunger?"

"Please don't distract me."

"You're going to have a hard time finding this one, especially with that stick. I buried it extra deep this time."

"Why, Eck? That isn't the point."

Eck didn't believe in imitation. Instead, she would steal plungers from unsuspecting Plumbesses, until eventually they all suspected her. Seg didn't know what Eck tried to do with the plungers, and she didn't want to know. Whenever Eck was found again, which always proved difficult, nothing ever seemed damaged. Roc, in such instances, would volunteer to deal punishment, especially when the plunger had been her own.

"Stop coddling her, Zag. Take that, you miscreant! That'll teach you to touch my plunger. Is nothing sacred?"

Seg had many dreams in which all she needed was a plunger but she never had one. Villages would flood, children would go missing, and the peasantry would come to her begging for help. "I can't," she'd say, over and over again. "I can't."

The dreams became so strangely traumatic that they reshaped her waking resolve. She decided, once and for all, to prove her worth; to delve so deeply into her studies that the Plumbesses would have to acknowledge her prowess. To stop hiding. And even to listen to Roc every now and then.

THE PLUNGER
[AGE 13]

WHEN THE TIME finally came, when the words, "Oh, you'll get your plunger, all right" finally parted Roc's arid mouth, Seg was surprised to find herself at the Hall of Water Closets, firmly in the Middle of the Incline.

"Why here?" Seg asked Roc.

"Where did you think we'd give you your plunger?" the Plumbess answered.

"Somewhere . . . cleaner? Somewhere farther up the Incline."

"Ha! Farther up the Incline? You think if I hand you this thing, you'll be a Plumbess, girl?" Roc looked down at the second plunger she held, nearly identical to her own, with a look of disgust. "You have years to go, girl. Still plenty of time for you to fail."

"Will that one be mine?" Seg asked, an admittedly

superfluous question. She'd been waiting so long that the possibility didn't seem real.

"It most certainly isn't mine."

They were waiting for Zag and Eck. As with every other momentous step in her apprenticeship, the Plumbesses wanted Eck there to ruin it for Seg, to copy her effort or scar her, or both. They'd been waiting for nearly half an hour, almost entirely in silence.

In her boredom, Seg opened the door to one of the water closets. Although she had put its cleanliness into doubt when arguing with Roc, in reality it was spotless. It didn't surprise Seg—a Plumbess wouldn't allow anything in the Orphanage to be dirty, even the most forlorn of orphans. The porcelain shined with eerie whiteness and the burnished copper connected everything with majestic purpose.

Behind her, Roc said, "Ever seen a toilet before?"

"Of course, Plumbess." Seg wouldn't give in to her provocations, not on the day she would receive her plunger.

Just then, Zag arrived, huffing, with Eck in tow. "Sorry, very sorry. She chose today, of all days, to go hiding on me. Found her in an irrigation ditch, and only because I saw half the field was dry and tried to fix it. *She* was the clog. You'd think she'd be excited—I told her she'd get her plunger today and she said, 'Yay,' but of course there's no telling with the girl."

Eck stood there, a strange smile on her face and showing obvious signs of irrigation. "Hi, Seg," she said.

Seg didn't reply.

"Well, let's get started, then," Roc said. "I'll take these four closets, you take those."

"Works for me," Zag said.

Roc dragged Seg into the nearest water closet and shut the door after them. Seg was unnerved by the sudden separation. "Why did they go to a different room?" she asked. "I thought they'd be doing this with us. I thought that's why we waited."

"First you complain about Eck being around, then you wonder why she isn't here. Don't worry your pretty little head—they're right on the other side of this wall. But this moment is private, this moment is between a Plumbess and her apprentice. Now, Seg, do you know why you're here?"

"To get my plunger," she replied firmly.

"No, girl. To find out what *Plumbing* really is. A Plumbess isn't her plunger, and she isn't that outfit you're wearing. A Plumbess isn't just some servant to be called on when the toilet's clogged, either, although don't worry—there'll be plenty of toilets. A Plumbess is a human embodiment of Plumbing. Now do you know where the word *Plumbing* comes from?"

Seg shook her head, agitated. "No. You haven't told me."

"I'm telling you now. It comes from an old language, from the word *plumbum*, which means lead. You're far too young to trust with lead now, but when you're Certified, we'll give it to you—a necklace, one kilogram, to wear around your neck at all times. That will mark you for what you are, and show you the real weight of Plumbing."

"I've never seen a Plumbess wear a necklace like that." In fact, one kilogram seemed like it would break Roc's thin, bird-like neck clean in half.

"There's a reason for that."

Seg waited to hear that reason, but it never came.

"Now, little girl, do you know why your name is Seg?"

An anger filled her, one she could never repress. "How

107

should I know? You've refused to tell me anything about my parents."

"What are you talking about, girl, and what makes you think you can use that tone with me? *I* named you. This has nothing to do with your parents."

The revelation sent Seg into shock. For her entire life she'd been under the impression that she had at least that one tenuous link to her faceless parents—that they had named her. To have that link not only shattered but replaced by Roc was more than she could take.

Roc continued without her. "The most important thing about a Plumbess is that she is a Plumbess. A beacon of light and cleanliness holding this miserable world together. Your name will never overshadow that. So it's three letters, and a single syllable. The most important part about you, Seg, won't be where you came from, or who your parents were, or anything about you. I've tried getting that through to you, but of course you're an obstinate little thing. Look at me. Stop crying. When you leave the Orphanage, you'll be a Plumbess. Plumbess Seg. And you'll do your work and find your orphan and come back to complete the cycle."

Seg hadn't forgotten the words spoken by Roc years ago, on the day Eck arrived—she'd said she was wasting her life on Seg, there at the Orphanage. The words still cut after so long.

"Are you going to give me my plunger now?" Seg asked, the firmness of her voice belied by the tears she couldn't help crying.

Roc looked at her as if at a loss, though naturally tending toward severity. Then she said, "You won't leave this room until this toilet's unclogged. And then there's three more. After those four toilets are dealt with, you can take your plunger and leave. If you think you're ready for it, take off your right glove."

Seg did as instructed, slipping the black glove from her diminutive wrist.

"Take my hand." The Plumbess held out her right hand, Seg's plunger clutched in its gnarled fingers.

Moderately confused, Seg placed her bare hand over the hand of the Plumbess.

Roc lifted her hand and then lowered it in the motion of the holy sign, pulling Seg's with it. Somewhere along the pipe of the holy sign, the plunger transferred from Roc's hand to the hand of her apprentice. Seg stared down at it, reverence sublimating in her heart. It was more than a stick—she could feel that right away.

"Now unclog that toilet, orphan."

Seg approached the toilet, which showed no signs of being clogged. Impulsively Seg pulled on the flushing valve, which sent water from a reservoir above their heads crashing down, immediately overfilling the toilet and pouring out onto the floor.

"Get plunging, girl!"

Seg thrust her plunger in, but it did little more than splash water around. "It's not working," she said.

"You've got to be angry, girl. I know you have it in you, you sulking little thing. Put it to good use for once."

Seg rooted around some more with her plunger until finally she encountered some resistance. Anger, she thought. Anger like being deceived about where her name came from. She thrust hard, and felt the clog dislodge. She operated the flushing valve again, and this time it cleared.

"Finally. On to the next one, then. Hopefully we won't be here all night."

Roc took her to the second water closet, and this one was obviously clogged. Seg gave the toilet a wide berth, disgusted by what she could smell and see.

Roc mocked her. "What did you think, girl, that it would be all flowers and sunshine? Get in there and plunge."

Reluctantly Seg approached the toilet and submitted her new plunger. She distanced her mind, thinking about happier days in happier places. She thought about Zag. She tried a few plunges, but nothing happened. She tried again, and in various ways, but to no effect.

Roc waited an hour before offering any advice. "Stop holding your breath. You're plunging a toilet, not diving into it."

Seg hadn't even realized she was holding her breath. "Tell me what to do, then."

"I've already told you. Anger, girl. And only anger. You can't be disgusted by what you're working with. Believe me, there are things out there much worse than human excrement. If you're disgusted, you'll hold part of yourself back. You need all of you."

Seg could understand the logic, but had a hard time implementing. She thought about all the things she'd revered plungers for—their majesty, their ability to heal people, their utility in *cooking*. "This can't possibly be what a plunger is for," she said.

"Don't deceive yourself. At the heart of all the things a plunger can fix is an Obstruction. If you can't face that Obstruction in its simplest form, you won't get very far. Now are you going to unclog this toilet or aren't you?"

Seg's anger flared again, but instead of channeling it into plunging, she struck the toilet with her plunger like it was a misbehaving child. And to Seg and Roc's mutual surprise, the toilet flushed itself. Roc peered down into the bowl, still in disbelief. She flushed it again, just to be sure.

"Bet you couldn't do that again if you tried," she finally said, and then took Seg to the third water closet.

Apparently Plumbesses were more lax about cleanliness than Seg thought, because the third water closet was so dirty that even the floors, walls, and ceiling were smeared with filth. Seg was already gagging in the hallway outside. Roc pushed her in from behind.

"How could a human even make a mess like this?" Seg asked, confounded.

"If you must know," Roc replied, giving her the rare, indirect answer, "this isn't entirely human. The point is that it's difficult to deal with. Now deal with it."

In a few minutes, Seg's senses were mostly deadened; it was finding firm footing that proved hardest. She tried the simple approach again—simply striking the toilet—and to her chagrin Roc was right: she couldn't do it again. So she plunged, and struggled to keep her mind present.

It was a fleeting thought about Eck, for some reason, that finally gave her the force to clear the toilet. Several hours had passed—the time was well past dinner, but Seg was in no way hungry.

"By the gods, I thought I'd die here of old age. Come along." The Plumbess pushed the door open and they went out into the hallway, toward the fourth and final water closet.

As it happened, Eck and Zag were in the hallway. Roc

asked, "Is yours giving you as much trouble as mine?"

Zag was never so quick to criticize. "Well, I had a hard time convincing her to use the head of her plunger—she kept wanting to plunge with the handle, like she wanted to stab the clogs out—but after a while I finally got her to turn it around. After that she did really well, I should say. Just finished."

Seg couldn't believe it. Eck had beaten her. The snake stood there, plunger held the wrong way over her shoulder, absolutely filthy, smiling as only she could. Seg hated her.

"Well, don't wait for us," Roc said. "We've got one more to go, and I imagine it'll take a while."

"You'll do fine, Seg," Zag said. "I believe in you." Then she left, with Eck straggling behind. Seg was truly alone with Roc.

Roc trudged over to the fourth door and pulled it open. This time it wasn't even lit—just a dark abyss exuding such a smell of filth and Obstruction that Seg couldn't process the signal. This time, instead of shoving Seg in ahead of her, Roc stepped in first and then turned to extend a hand out to Seg.

Whether to validate Zag's belief in her or to spite Roc and Eck, Seg took the proffered hand and entered the fourth water closet.

Four hours later, Seg was lying in her bed, plunger by her side—washed, of course. It would be her last night in the apprentice dormitory; then she'd have her own room right below the Top of the Incline. So much effort just to climb a hill.

Eck was already asleep next to her. The girl was wrapped so tightly in her sheets that it looked like she should asphyxiate. Seg thought about waking her, to show her that she too was worthy of a plunger, but decided to wait until morning.

Seg returned to her dreams triumphant, a plunger in her

hands. People came to her, the same people and the same problems she'd been plagued with for years. But this time she had an answer, only slightly tainted by her time in the water closets.

A woman came to her, tearing her hair out in handfuls. She said, "I've lost my baby."

"Where did you lose her?" Seg asked.

"In the storm." The woman pointed to the broad horizon, a cataclysm of storms that never ended.

"That's not somewhere to take a child," Seg chided.

"Please, help her."

Seg set off on her journey, which only took a few moments. The storms opened up around her—every raindrop was an evanescent pipe connecting heaven and earth. At the storm's edge, at the very spot where another step would have cost her life, she tested the power of her plunger. With more than enough anger at a mother neglectful enough to lose a child, she struck the rain itself, shattering the pipes and granting her passage inward.

"I can be a Plumbess," she said. And she broke forward, through thousands and thousands of pipes, an unstoppable force, her anger only growing until she reached an eye to the storm.

A man stood in its middle, wearing a raincoat and top hat but completely dry. All that was visible of his face was a wicked grin.

"I know you have the child," she yelled at him. "Give her back."

His eyes lifted, revealing liquid gold. They burned into Seg, causing her to falter. He laughed once and a sudden torrent of rain fell down at her, solid copper pipes that threatened to pierce her through.

She lashed out, but she was desperate now. Every pipe she deflected shattered and poured its content all over her. Soon she was drowning, the water and pipes all around her. Flailing, she let go of her plunger and grabbed her own neck.

Several terrifying seconds went by before she realized that she was actually awake, and still drowning, surrounded on all sides by water. Something latched around her wrist and tried pulling it, but she struggled against it with all her remaining strength. It persisted—it was so tight that soon her hand became numb—and finally it pulled with such sudden force that Seg was pulled with it, her head striking a hard object and leaving her completely disoriented.

Then she broke the surface, and realized it was Eck who held on to her. The girl was treading the dorm room's flooded waters, carrying Seg's dead weight.

"Come on, Seg, this way," Eck said, and pulled her along.

The next morning revealed the full extent of the damage. A water main had broken, unloading its massive capacity directly into the apprentice dormitory. Somehow no one had died, but half of the Incline showed scars from the runoff. For two days Seg sat on a bench in silence and watched the cleanup.

Seg had caused the rupture, in her struggle against the nightmare. The Plumbesses called it a pipe dream and told her to learn from it—whatever that meant. For the most part she was left alone in her sullen contemplation, although Roc came by and frowned at her, and even Eck tried to give her a word or two of serpentine comfort.

It was Zag who finally caused her to break her silence. The

soft Plumbess sat by her side and stared down the Incline with her at what was left of the damage.

Seg spoke first. "I think Eck saved me."

The Plumbess just nodded. They watched for a while as servants rebuilt a garden terrace.

Then Seg asked the question that had weighed on her the most for those two days. "If a plunger is so dangerous, why give it to a child? Why give it to me?"

Zag smiled, something rare since whatever she'd found at the end of Eck's shower drain. She said, "Roc saw something in you, Seg, otherwise she never would've taken you in. And I, I saw the same thing in Eck. Maybe you can see it yourself better now—she's got goodness in her. You do too. And it is goodness that must take the plunger firmly in its hand."

"But the risk . . . "

"The risk," Zag repeated slowly. "Yes, the risk. Let me show you something—something I haven't shown anyone else."

To Seg's surprise, the Plumbess pulled up the hem of her pants, exposing her right leg all the way up to the thigh. It was covered in scars, some wide and sweeping, others small and circular.

"You're not the only one who's been bitten. You wouldn't believe how many snakes I had to wade through to get to Eck. Enormous snakes, snakes like I'd never seen before. I could only protect so much of myself with my plunger—they got my legs pretty good, and my stomach a few times. I probably nearly died. But she was starving, Seg. I couldn't just leave her like that, a helpless child. She would've died. And my point is—one of these days, Seg, you'll save someone yourself. And you'll realize that it was worth every risk you took."

THE DRY PRINCESS

TWICE A DAY court was held, an hour each time. Twice a day Marcus would sit in his useless golden throne, his back to the Fountain, and look down upon his court, the upper echelons of Manor society ordered by rank and merit. The barons and baronesses were always invited, and occasionally some engineer men or doctors when technical matters were discussed. Peasants were only allowed under extreme circumstances.

Twice a day Eck stood to Marcus's left and tried not to say anything. It was a generally difficult experience—not so much the silence, but sometimes her opinion was called on, and she had to give a few words in the name of Plumbing. Worse was before and after the court sessions, when etiquette transformed by slow degrees into gossip. The Dry Princess was a common theme, whoever she was, but the incident with

Baron Marlow at the ball was gaining traction.

On the fourth day after the ball, a baroness went so far as to ask Marcus about the matter directly. She waited until after court, which had involved a speech by Baron Cress on the benefits of social pruning. A large number of the court were still around, and they barely concealed their interest as the conversation developed.

"I've had it, simply had it, my lord," she began.

"With what?" Marcus asked, a calm smile on his face.

"I must know what the Plumbess did to our Baron Marlow so that a doctor can fix it. He's broken, just completely snapped. He only talks about moths, and he won't touch any doors. A servant has to let him out of his chambers every morning, and I've half a mind to tell them just to leave him confined in there. It reflects poorly on all of us, one of our own walking around making moth talk."

"Ha!" Marcus exclaimed. "If you ask me, it sounds like he got what he deserves. That will teach him to touch my Plumbess."

"A humble request, Pipe Lord," the baroness replied.

"Plumbess," Marcus said.

"What?"

"Could you tell the lovely Baroness Elsipa what you did to Baron Marlow, so that she might know peace?"

"I believe," Eck said, in much of a whisper, "that I attached his drain to his source."

"There you have it," Marcus said, much louder than Eck. "Drain to his source. The matter is settled."

"But—"

"Excuse me, baroness, but you got what you asked for, and

as it so happens I have more important matters to attend to."

As the baroness huffed off, Marcus said to Eck so that only she could hear, "Plumbess, I believe it's time we put you to work. As you might have heard, the Dry Princess is coming. She'll be here in two days, in fact."

"I've heard something like that," Eck replied, nodding.

"Then you know what that means," he said.

"No, no I don't. I'd never heard of her before."

"Oh . . . they really don't tell you much about the broader world there in your Orphanage, do they. No matter. The Dry Princess . . . you see, sometimes she travels to a city like ours to mercilessly tempt one of the Pipe Lords. And we, for our part, turn off all the water while she visits. She simply detests water. She won't even enter a city if we've got it flowing somewhere, which is a shame because you know how splendid the Fountain is."

Eck nodded. That was finally a truth she felt confident about.

"And so I'd like you to get familiar with our valves, so you can turn them off. But we'll need to do more than shut the valves off to get ready. The library, you see, flooded just the day before you arrived. I've heard rumors that books still float up into the toilets every now and then. I'm afraid that if the Dry Princess so much as hears about a wet library, she'll avoid our city entirely. So that's the nature of it, what I'm calling your first task. Make the Manor presentable for the Dry Princess."

"Okay," Eck said. "Yes, I can do that. Valves and library."

"Best of luck."

Although the task seemed strange, Eck was more than glad to be leaving the court and turning to Plumbing. Whoever the

Dry Princess was, she sounded to Eck like a horrible person. In fact, it defied everything Eck knew about humanity that a person would detest water. The woman must've smelled horrible, at the very least.

Eck returned first to her garden, to prepare. She already had her plunger with her—she hadn't let it from her hand since the incident with Baron Marlow—and she was already in her Plumbess outfit, but she wanted her snakes as well.

"Shash!" she called out into the wooded portion of her room. "Perceval! Dennis! Come to me! We have a mission, let's go!" As the snakes slithered up to her, she stuffed them into her bag. "Stay quiet," she warned them. "People around here don't like you."

Satisfied, she went to search out the head engineer man, who she'd met just the day before. He'd given a speech at the second court about the inherent sadness of pipes, and seemed to think he knew a lot about Plumbing, all of which caused Eck to laugh the entire time. The people around her, Marcus included, didn't seem to share her humor. She found him near the Hall of Water Closets with an important look on his face.

"I have a mission, Plumber man," she said when she saw him—it was a joke of a title, stolen from the servant who asserted that the engineer men deserved it. Using a joke like that was as close as she came to condescension, but it felt appropriate for him. "I must fix your library, but I don't know where it is. And I must shut off your valves—the Dry Princess is coming."

He met the first sentence with indifference and the second with severe reverence. "Yes, the Dry Princess," he said. "It's unfortunate to be a man of such low station when royalty like that exists in the world."

"It's unfortunate to be a man at all," she replied. "Now come on!"

Begrudgingly he led the way. As she followed, Eck rediscovered a fact that she'd recently unlearned: the layout of the Manor, despite its occasional poorly Plumbed hallway or room, was in fact very similar to the Orphanage—at least in the respect that the Manor, the most important of its parts, was prominent in the center, like the Incline, and the lesser buildings tapered off below it. Of course, the Orphanage library was on the Top of the Incline, and the engineer man led her to where the Plumbesses would have housed the servants. Still, the similarities were striking.

The library turned out to be a lake with a roof of an island stranded in its middle. "This is it," the engineer man announced. "Now what are you going to do about it?"

"Fix it, of course. What have you done to the place?"

"We put berms up to contain it," he replied. "To contain the damage."

"And what did you intend to do next?" she asked.

"Given enough time, it'll dry up on its own. Then we'd restructure the terrain with ditches, drains, all that, so the water flows elsewhere. But I can see already that the Plumbess isn't impressed. What would _you_ do?"

Eck had been violently shaking her head. "If you've got a place that collects water so well, you should let it. Use it."

"It's a library, Plumbess. Generally we'd like to keep the books dry."

"They sound like a certain princess I've heard strange things about. But really, if you're so worried about the books, you'd be better off covering them in crystal like you did to your gardens. That would be much less work than changing all this topography. You'd have to dig a river to keep this dry— this is nothing that a blind drain or two could fix."

"Tell me then, wise Plumbess, what you would do. I'm just an engineer."

"Talk to it."

"Talk to it?"

"Naturally." She began wading into the library's lake, her black rubber boots more than equal to the task.

The engineer man hesitated at the bank. "Plumbess . . . "

"If you're afraid of ruining your pretty shoes"—that made Eck laugh—"then just stay where you are. I can take care of this myself."

He looked ashamed, but stayed where he was. She waded deeper, until eventually she had to swim to proceed.

It was difficult, but she forced herself through one of the submerged windows. Inside was a water maze of bookshelves complicated by floating books. It was dark—there were sconces on the walls, but all of them had long since burned down or been extinguished. She surfaced and swam onward, toward the center, where she expected to find—a fountain.

She knew it. Even if the engineer man claimed the library was a "dry" place, whoever designed it couldn't help but center it around a poor imitation of the real Fountain. She swam a circle around it, trying to find the best point of ingress.

"Right there," she said to a thick, exposed pipe that had exuded water on better days. It was wide enough for a snake.

She whispered instructions to Shash, and then deposited him into the pipe. She listened for a moment to the sounds of him slithering down, and then said to the rest of the snakes,

"It's going to be hard to sleep in here, don't you think? But we'll find someplace nice."

She continued into the labyrinth, swimming by countless books. She read the titles of a few of them as they passed, following some secret current, but they were never anything good—mostly poetry. "The Plumbing books are too smart to get caught up in a mess like this," she told her snakes, safe on her back. "They'll be somewhere dry."

Eventually, she found what she was looking for—a floating couch very close to an underwater hearth. Of course there was no flame, but even drowned it radiated a warmth of sorts. She clambered onto the couch, which threatened more than once to capsize. Settled, she hummed soft songs to herself, simple pipe organ that she was, as the couch swayed gently on the waves. Before she knew it, she was asleep.

In the dream, she sat up from her reclined position. The couch was firmly on the ground, the hearth filled with a healthy flame. The sconces too were lit, revealing a deceptively dry library, quiet and orderly, with all its books properly shelved. "You're lying to yourself," she told it, but of course it didn't respond. She stood up and made her way back to the fountain.

Where the fountain had been was Shash, wound to a height of three meters and bubbling water from his mouth, which traced its way down his scales and disappeared somewhere in the center of his coil. "Shash!" she yelled at him. "Stop being a fountain! We need a drain!"

The snake listened. Water stopped pouring from his mouth, and he rose to as high as the library ceiling would allow and then struck the ground below him, with such force that many of the books were shaken back off their shelves.

The place where the fountain had been was now a gaping hole, its bottom unfathomable. Into it, she proclaimed, "Library, I've given you a drain. I recommend you use it. If you don't, the Plumber man might take some drastic measures to change you."

Suddenly the colors started draining out around her, the light from the sconces and her breath itself. They formed a whirlpool that centered around the drain that was once a fountain. Soon it was pitch black, a darkness that threatened all life. Eck woke before it was too late.

She was on the couch again, but the hearth was unlit. She lowered her feet to the ground, to the carpet sopping there. "Good library," she said. She gathered up Shash, shelved one or two of the thousands of books strewn around, and exited the library.

Outside, the engineer man was firmly astounded. "What did you do?" he asked.

"I did what I said I would. I talked to it. And gave it a drain, I suppose. But it had to be convinced to use it. I can't control buildings."

He didn't seem to take much from her explanation. "You used your plunger," he said. "That's why I couldn't do the same thing myself. I don't have a plunger."

It was only then that she realized she hadn't, in fact, used her plunger. That was a problem—a Plumbess should use her plunger. That was what a Plumbess did. She'd have to remember that for the next time. "Stop gawking, Plumber man, and show me your valves. We're only halfway done here."

"Of course. Right this way."

Eck was disappointed, but not surprised, to find the valves

housed in an ignominious shed of sorts, leaning against the back of the Manor. At the Orphanage, the valves were displayed even more proudly than the pipes themselves. Yet another thing to shake her worldview of what should and shouldn't be.

The valve house currently had four engineer men in it, going about their daily inspections and preventative maintenance. With the addition of Eck and the head engineer man, the room was nearly to capacity. "Do you know what that is?" he asked, pointing to an intricate metal machine hooked directly up to a lead pipe.

She shook her head.

"A pipegram. A pipe that goes all the way to the Orphanage."

"Oh." At first she was impressed, but then she realized it was a pipe very similar to the one that had driven her and Seg apart. Not wishing to display emotions, she said, "The valves, Plumber man."

"Right over here."

Two engineer men vacated enough space for Eck to get a good view of them: row after row of valves. The head engineer man said, "So I'll start with this one right here. This valve—"

"Don't tell me," she interjected, and struck the valve's adjoining pipe with her plunger. She tilted her head to the side, listening for something. And for once, she heard what she was looking for. "The bathroom sinks on the second floor?"

Again, he seemed amazed beyond belief, looking distractedly at her plunger. But then his face contorted into an emotion that Eck couldn't recognize. "If you don't need me,

Plumbess, then I'll just be on my way."

"No, please," she said. "I probably couldn't do that again. I would appreciate it if you explained the other valves to me."

Moderately placated, the engineer man gave the number and function for every valve he was familiar with, which was about three hundred of the four hundred fifty-seven. Eck didn't mind the omissions—she felt like she could extrapolate the rest, which the engineer man had declared less important anyway.

"I suppose I'll start with this one," she said after he finished, and reached out for one of the ten valves that operated the Fountain.

She'd nearly turned it when the engineer man said, clearly afraid, "What are you doing?"

"Marcus told me to turn off the water," she said, confounded. "For the Dry Princess."

"No, not today. He wouldn't have told you to do it today. We'll close it right before she arrives, and we'll open it right after she leaves. That's the only way."

" . . . Why?"

"The last time we turned off the Fountain, just for two hours to do some standard maintenance, we lost the library. And that was with hours of planning."

"I fixed the library. This valve—"

"Now I might not be a Plumbess like you, and I might not understand why floods happen every time we so much as look at some of these valves, but I have a lot of practical experience with this system. I think that should count for something. And I know for a fact that this visit of the Dry Princess is going to cost us something, and I hate to think what. So will you listen to me or won't you?"

She looked him over for a moment—proud, defiant, expecting her to plunge onward without regarding him in the least. It was the first time she'd seen him so clearly. "I—I'm sorry. I'll do as you say. We didn't have so much water to worry about at the Orphanage. If you turned off a valve, that was it. I'm sure there's a lot you know about the Manor and its Plumbing that would benefit me greatly if you told me. Would you like to?"

Her simple admission and request changed the head engineer man completely, to the point where she didn't recognize him again. He took her all over the Manor, pointing out pipes large and small and talking about incidents from years before. And she listened to everything, not interrupting him once—even when the Plumbing became a bit questionable.

She discovered that he didn't know much about how the sky and river were bound—the former Plumbess had excluded his company—but he knew enough about how to mitigate the problems they caused. When she asked if Marcus would know more, he replied, "The Pipe Lord knows nothing about what we do." Reflecting on their walk in the garden, Eck was inclined to believe him.

Two days later, when the Dry Princess arrived, it was Eck herself who shut off all the valves. There was a very specific sequence that needed to be followed, otherwise pipes would burst or pumps would break. The head engineer man watched her work, looking like he wanted her to fail.

She made sure to disappoint him.

"That was . . . well done, Plumbess," he said when all the valves were finally closed.

Because the main gate into the Manor of Storms was right

next to where the river was eaten alive—Eck offered to shut down the whole operation, but Marcus declined—the Dry Princess and her retinue entered from the north gate, which happened to be a lot smaller.

The majesty of the procession was only slightly compromised—bannermen entered first, carrying flags of leather so cracked that they didn't say anything at all. They were followed by carriages of sand, which continuously leaked out into the street. The expectant crowd, gathered tightly to both sides, picked up handfuls of the sand and threw it jubilantly in the air, where it quickly became a choking hazard. The Pipe Lord and his Plumbess stood at the base of the motionless Fountain, surrounded by attendants.

The carriages were pulled by the most pathetic horses Eck had ever seen. Out of commiseration with snakes, she'd never once felt empathy for a horse, but still she felt compelled to ask Marcus, "What's wrong with them?"

Marcus startled, as if broken from some reverie. "Wrong with who? Oh, the horses? Yes, the entire time they're under the employ of the Dry Princess, they're not given water. As you might expect, a lot of them die. When the Dry Princess leaves, *if* the Dry Princess leaves, she'll expect replacements from our stables for all the horses lost on her journey here."

And, in fact, one of the horses did collapse right in the middle of the street, upsetting its carriage and spreading a fog of sand around it. The impact of the horse itself caused no sound—when the dust finally settled, its pronounced ribcage was clearly immobile.

"That's the most horrible thing I've ever seen," said the orphan who'd stared into abysses darker than any ever seen by a Plumbess.

"Royalty can go to excesses sometimes," said the man who had bound sky and earth to feed the Fountain.

Although the procession as a whole was delayed by the upset carriage, the Dry Princess herself was unstoppable—she was carried in a palanquin by men so dehydrated they didn't even sweat, who were able to skirt the carriage and dead horse and deposit their royal burden at the base of the staircase that led to the Fountain.

She emerged with a rigid grace that could only be described as dry, into a world of moisture she clearly despised. Her clothes covered her modestly, but were made of what looked like thin paper crackling in the wind, so brittle that they might break at any moment. Her hair, on the other hand, seemed as rigid as clay after a kiln, and stood motionless in the sky.

She took the first stair and gave a cracked smile. She whispered what should have been "Pipe Lord Marcus," but her lips seemed to lack the sufficient moisture to make a *p* sound, so it came out as "High Lord Marcus," which only coincidentally still sounded respectful. "It's so nice to see you again."

Ten meters away, Marcus somehow guessed an appropriate reply. "You know that the pleasure is mine, princess."

A dry herald hurried up the stairs in front of her and proclaimed, hardly louder than the princess herself, "The princess has had a long journey, and will require sustenance. To eat she would prefer sand from the land of Barren, but will settle for a pork roast overcooked by two days. To drink she would prefer the spirits of men who have perished in the desert, but will settle for a sufficiently aged Chardonnay."

"See that it's done," Marcus said to the surrounding attendants. Half of them scattered.

Still only on the second stair, the Dry Princess gestured to the Fountain and said, "Such a large amount of metal for nothing, High Lord." She gave a knowing, wry smile.

Eck didn't know she knew. "It's the Fountain," she said. "Usually it has water flowing through it."

Even as a whisper, Marcus's reply to her was the harshest she'd ever received from him. "Please, Plumbess, don't mention water around the Dry Princess again."

The Dry Princess, apparently a performer of sorts, made a show of fainting and had to start from the bottom of the stairs again. A few minutes later, she was close enough to comment on the event that upset her so. "A 'Lumbess, Marcus?"

"You know very well, princess, that if you graced me with your permanent presence I would gladly do without."

That earned another smile from the princess. Eck, for her part, was taken aback. Not only because of Marcus's comment, but because of the princess's skin, which was finally close enough to make out clearly. It was mottled red, covered in lesions and chafed at the joints.

She asked Marcus, loudly enough for anyone and everyone to hear, "What's wrong with her skin? I expected her to smell, but I didn't expect her to look this terrible."

His voice replied rather thinly. "My dear Eck, if you could please excuse us. The Dry Princess and I could use some time alone."

Eck might have been offended, but she had a more important matter to attend to herself. She quickly walked away, down the staircase to where the Dry Princess's horses were being unharnessed by dry men and transferred to the stablemen of the Manor.

To a dry man, she said, "Please allow me to take the horses around to the river where they can get a drink. There's no water"—the dry man flinched—"at the stable."

A stableman behind her, struggling to keep a horse upright, said, "While under the employ of the Dry Princess, they can't—"

"Those are just words!" Eck yelled. "Let's just say they're under my employ for the moment, I'll give them water, and then when I'm done they can be under her employ or your employ or anyone else's employ. I don't care."

"I'm sorry, Plumbess," the stableman replied. "It doesn't work like that."

A similar mentality contaminated her dinner that night, which she was forced to share with the engineer men. It was the first meal she hadn't eaten with Marcus since arriving at the Manor.

They ate the jerky of some gamey animal—probably horse—and shamefully passed around a water skin. Whenever someone took a drink, everyone averted their eyes like they were taking part in a communal sin.

Finally she'd had enough, and stood up to throw her jerky in the face of a grimacing man. "It's just water!" she yelled. "I thought you were engineer men. I thought you admired Plumbing!"

"You wouldn't understand, Plumbess. She's the Dry Princess."

She continued yelling. "What makes you think I wouldn't understand that?" Then she left them.

That night, huddled under her favorite bush, Eck had a hard time finding sleep. When she finally did, she had dreams

of flowing water, and they weighed so heavily on her conscience that she woke up again. It was sometime in the very
early morning, several hours before dawn. She got up and
dressed herself.

When she tried opening the door of her garden to leave,
she found it valveless. Frustrated, she struck it with her plunger, confident that she just had to unblock it. Nothing happened. "Agh! This door isn't a valve at all!" she yelled, and
sulked back to her bush.

She found Dennis there. "Dennis, show me a drain so I can
get out of here."

The snake took her to a small drain next to some daisies.

"Narrow, but I think I can make it. Lead the way, Dennis."

Outside, she struggled to retrace the path to the valve
house. Eventually she made it without incident. In the light of
a crescent moon, she read valve numbers until she found the
forty-ninth. Without any hesitation, she opened it.

In a darker humor, she found valve number two hundred
thirty-one. That one supplied the room that would be the Dry
Princess's chambers for the night, and probably would have
done her skin a world of good. That one she hesitated with,
her hand on the valve and her heart racing. In the end, though,
she left it closed.

She struggled again through the darkness, this time to
find the stable. Simply turning the valve on in the valve house
wouldn't suffice—there was another valve in the stable itself.
She found a trail of sand that fortunately led her to the right
place. There she filled a trough, and then carefully woke the
horses so they wouldn't make too much noise.

Several of the horses she had to forcefully teach how to

drink, as they seemed to have forgotten. But eventually they all joined in. To one in particular, head fully submerged in the trough, she said, "I'm trusting you to drain this entire thing before morning so no one suspects me, okay?"

He probably didn't hear her.

VISCOSITY OF A CHILD

BARON SETH DID not allow himself to be simply stricken down by the Law—appeals were made and unmade, affidavits were written and unwritten, witnesses were called and uncalled. Several weeks went by, and nothing really changed.

The Law got close—a particularly damning piece of evidence came to light, namely that Baron Seth had in fact pledged his river to the city some forty years earlier in no uncertain terms. In response, however, Baron Seth made an elaborate case for the unsoundness of his mind at the time of the contract, implicating both his naïve youth and the treacherous course of time itself. He then nearly lost his river again when his unsoundness was not only accepted but applied to his current state, Gregor making the argument that a river owned by an unsound mind could destroy, possibly, the very fabric of existence. But then Baron Seth countered with a brutal tirade about how he'd never seen anything clearer, the men around

133

him unfit of rank or title, the carrion eaters, the way a Law-abiding gentleman might be ripped limb from limb. After that, the trial was roughly where it started.

During every recess the Pipe Lord's Hose was brought out and the peasantry watered, usually by Seg herself. That was the largest part of her contribution to the trial—only three times was she called on to testify, once on a matter of Plumbing, which she deftly answered, and twice to support moral accusations against Baron Seth, which she handled with considerable ambivalence. She didn't approve of the way Baron Seth deprived the city of such an important resource, but she also didn't approve of the way Gregor and the other barons made fatuous arguments, gainsaid anything, and bullied everyone. Because she didn't simply go along with it, they probably wouldn't ask her to testify again.

And yet she watched the trial anyway, from the peasant seats, because what Gregor had told her when she first arrived was true: a Plumbess without water didn't have much to do. At first she didn't believe that the river and the abysmal Well were the only water in a city so large. So many nearby villages had said the same, and with a strike of her plunger she had proven them wrong, finding water where it was never expected. But Hope Springs truly was as barren as it looked. So, she watched a pointless trial drag on into infinity.

Until, one day, something finally happened. She was sitting in a closet with Carral—he often took her there when he wanted a task done, but he always forgot what the task was, so she would just sit in silence for a while as the old man breathed heavily—when someone flung the closet door open.

It was Samuel, the one and only engineer of Hope Springs.

He said, "Pipe Lord, I'm glad I found you. I've got two rather important messages for you."

"Well, boy," Carral said, "get on with it. Can't you see we're busy?"

"Of course, my lord. The first is that I got word from Sail's Reach—relayed through the Orphanage, so gods know how accurate it is—that not very long ago the Dry Princess visited the Manor of Storms. No word if she stayed or not, but she was there."

"My goodness," Carral said. The clouds in his eyes were replaced by sharper ones—still clouded, but differently. "The Dry Princess . . . "

"Who's that?" Seg asked. She'd never heard of her, but someone with the title of princess had to be important.

"When I was a young lad," Carral began, perhaps on his way to answer the question and perhaps not, "I was very ambitious. I wanted everything, like any sensible person would. And then my father handed me the pipe and died, and then I was Pipe Lord of Hope Springs, you understand? So many natural resources, but unused, untapped. I was ready to build. The Dry Princess, you see—when I was even younger, oh-so young, I thought she was a myth. They said she'd been wandering the deserts for centuries, looking for a man worthy of her. What kind of woman waits that long?

"But when she does find a worthy man, a Pipe Lord, and marries him—I don't know the results of such a union, but I've dreamed about them—that man will be the Pipe King. He will control Plumbing itself, and people will flow wherever he says. He'll have the Dry Queen by his side, guiding and steadying his hand. Too good to be true, you might say. I thought so myself. But then I saw her with my very own eyes, and I was convinced. Beauty beyond compare. I had to impress her.

"She's only impressed, you see, only attracted by, power. But she also won't stand to be *near* such power. A humming-bird made out of glass, the Dry Princess. So, the aspiring man must be gentle but merciless, the most powerful but power-less—in short, an impossible balance between mutually exclu-sive forces. I was ready to try.

"And that's when Plumbess Mar came to me. She was . . . she was everything I needed to get everything I wanted. And she was willing to help me with my dream, yes. She was ambi-tious too, you know. And so we forged grand plans, the grand-est. Things unheard of. And we started to build. But these things, these monumental endeavors, are too large for one life-time. The Plumbess and I, we got old and we died, our work unfinished.

"But it's not too late for Gregor. For the Dry Princess. And now you're here. If you could start where we left off, I'm sure you could finish it. Such . . . such grandeur, such power. The Dry Princess. I'd almost forgotten how badly I wanted her."

Samuel, also almost forgotten, said, "There's the other thing too, my lord. The second thing. A boy has fallen into the drain system."

Carral's clouds reversed, and he became again the con-fused, lost child he truly was, a blameless child that nothing could be expected from.

"Where?" Seg asked, taking the initiative in Carral's stead. "Take me there. Now."

As they walked, a Plumbess and an engineer, she asked pointed questions. Understandably, he didn't seem to want to answer any of them.

"Why would I know his name? A boy is a boy. He's a small thing, I can tell you that much. And his mother, I know his mother. She's nice." And, "I don't know much about the drain system. There's nothing to drain, so why should I?"

So when they arrived at a boarded-up cavern, Seg didn't know what to expect. Samuel said, "The boys, they like to come here sometimes and mess around, so we boarded it up. But you know boys—they get in anyway."

Seg could easily see how. The boards were low enough that she straddled them effortlessly and crossed to the other side.

"You coming too?" she asked the engineer, who deliberately moved no closer to the cavern.

"I'd rather not," he said.

"Fine, go. Leave me alone."

And soon she was. She walked deeper into the cavern, where no light crept, and approached the edge of an extraordinary pipe. Why was it so large? She tried hitting it with her plunger once or twice, Plumbing its depths, but the answer that returned was vague. And so she simply made a decision. A boy was down there somewhere, and every minute counted. She dove.

She fell for longer than she would've thought. Gradually the pipe became horizontal, and she transitioned from falling to sliding. Several times she had to make choices between right and left and up and down, when the pipe suddenly branched in the dark.

The surface of the pipe was rough from oxidation, and tore at her clothing. By the time she finally landed, at some depth she couldn't even fathom, her outfit was sheared off in several places. But for the most part she was uninjured, and quickly carried on.

It was so very dark, and the dryness of the drain made even Hope Springs seem humid. She tried calling out several times, yelling, "Boy!" since she didn't have a better name. The drain took the sound and disposed of it—not even an echo returned to her.

She tried to keep a mental map as she went farther in, with the intention of going farther down, but still she felt lost. Everything about the drain—its structure, its darkness—seemed foreign to her. And there was no sign of any boy.

She struck the pipe wall with her plunger and the section above her collapsed. She wasn't physically hurt, even though some fairly large clumps of earth fell on her. Mentally, though, she broke.

All at once terror bloomed inside of her, a barely repressed fear of drains that had always been with her. She became claustrophobic, and felt like she couldn't breathe. The Lead around her neck got heavier, and the wound of her scar opened. Frantically, and against her own intentions, she pushed herself free and retraced the path of her mental map back to the drain's entrance. When the pipe became too steep to walk on, she used her plunger to climb. Several hours later she was right back where she started, nothing gained. The boy was still down there.

It was nearly sunset. Ashamed of the state of her outfit, she first stopped at her own hovel to change into a spare. Then she walked down the depressing alley that led to Samuel's hovel, where she harshly knocked on the door.

The engineer answered. "Dead, right?" He had his arms conclusively folded like he had expected as much.

With her plunger she gave him a firm jab in the ribs, which caused him to gasp in pain.

"What was that for?" he asked.

"A reminder. The town you live in is called Hope Springs. Remember that."

"Peh," he said, but without conviction.

"Is there a schematic of the drain system? A blueprint? It's far more . . . complicated down there than I expected."

"I think there's something like that," he said, nodding. "A blueprint, drawn up by the old Plumbess. I've got it in the valve house. If you wait until tomorrow—"

"Thanks," she called back, already walking toward the valve house.

The sun had set by the time she reached it—fortunately, the exposed wall let in a lot of moonlight. She realized, not for the first time, that the valve house was a dirty place. There was an inexplicable number of chairs, all broken and scattered about. Short, pointless pieces of piping were here and there, and the trash of a thousand meals mortared the gaps, all probably eaten by Samuel and Samuel alone. She set about trying to find a blueprint in such a mess.

By luck, or some other guiding force, she found a small filing cabinet in what she'd thought was the nest of some large bird. Mixed in with instruction manuals, pamphlets, and notebooks with strange writings was a pair of blueprints, folded many times so they fit in the cabinet.

She cleared off a nearby table with a swipe of her plunger and then lit a candle to place at its edge. Then she laid the first blueprint out to its full breadth.

It showed, to the most minute of details, a spectacular water-supply system, drawn out with white chalk in precise lines. The whole system, she noticed, was centered around Baron

Seth's river, which it portrayed rather largely. It really must have changed, she decided. The scale seemed too accurate to get something like that wrong.

She took a very long moment to appreciate the other details: a well-placed infiltration basin, a thoughtful network of irrigation ditches, and two water towers that addressed the town from its wide sides. She nodded approvingly at all of it—this was a Plumbess, the artist of the blueprint, who understood water supply. And the signature at the bottom-right corner showed it as the work of Plumbess Mar.

It wasn't what Seg had come for, however, so she folded it up and put it into a pocket at her breast—she was confident it wouldn't be missed. Then she laid out the second of the blueprints, which revealed itself to be an equally extensive draining system.

She was much less capable of appreciating it, although she was still impressed. The drain went to extraordinary depths, but came back again. It was septic everywhere it needed to be and fast-flowing everywhere else, thousands of pipes splitting like the roots of a grand tree. It could have easily managed a thousand times the current population of Hope Springs. A drain large enough for the driest of princesses, Seg thought.

The hours slipped away as she stared at the blueprint, trying to make sense of its grand scope. The sun dawned on her at one point, and she remembered the urgency of her timeline. She folded that blueprint too, and placed it in her pocket with the first. Then she went to find the mother of the lost boy.

The mother turned out to be much easier to find. She'd taken her grief, as any mother would, straight to court, where she was yelling at the barons for their inaction and ineptitude. Simultaneously, a doctor—who claimed to be an expert on such things—was giving his testimony about the mental health of Baron Seth. The prognosis didn't seem good.

Damningly the mother yelled down at Carral, who shriveled under her wrath. "What have you done?"

"We've done something," he whispered.

"What? What have you done!?"

"I don't know! Something, though. Surely we've done something." He turned to the other barons for support.

Seg spared them further floundering. "I went down into the drain," she told the mother. "But I wasn't able to find him, not yet at least. I need to know more. Come with me and tell me about your boy."

The mother climbed down from the chair she'd been using as a pulpit. They left the courthouse, and behind them the testimony of the doctor continued uninterrupted.

From the start, Seg didn't like the woman. Anyone who could simply lose a child would have no empathy from her. And from what she'd seen at the courthouse, the mother seemed to think the barons, of all people, were responsible, not herself. Seg was quick to remind her of the reality of the matter.

"When did you lose him?" she asked.

"I didn't—"

"When."

"Er, last I saw him was second bell, I imagine. Yesterday. And the other boy, the boy he was with, came back and raised the alarm right before the third bell, I believe."

"What's your boy's name?" she asked.

"Does it matter?" the mother replied. "He's probably the only boy down there."

"If I have to repeat any more questions, I'll disembowel you, understood?" She sliced the air with her plunger for emphasis. "What is his name?"

"Eric," the mother said, looking a little shaken by the threat.

"And how old is he?"

"Just turned seven, I think."

"Would you say he's intelligent? Objectively?"

"He does all right for himself, but I don't see—"

"You're lucky you answered before digressing, or that would've been the end of you. If you must know, and really you mustn't, I need to know his variables—his density, his viscosity, all of that. And the mental variables, they matter as much as the physical ones. Do you know his dimensions? Height?"

"He has a twin, you know. You can look at him if you want."

"Are they similar?" Seg asked.

"They're twins," the mother replied.

"And we're both humans, yet your inability to just answer questions comes from some other species entirely. *Are they similar?*"

"Yes," the mother replied, guarding her bowels. "Yes."

They reached a hovel very similar to the hovel of the Pipe Lord. "I'll get him," the mother said. "Be right back."

In a few moments a twin was produced, and looked much as anticipated: a seven-year-old boy who, mentally, probably did all right for himself.

"I'd like to ask him some questions and take him around town for some experiments," Seg said.

"What are you going to do to him?"

"If you'd shown this much concern for his brother, we wouldn't be having this conversation. I'll return him by nightfall."

That settled the matter. Seg and the boy walked off, and she wasted no time proceeding to more questions.

She adopted a much softer tone than the one she'd used with the mother. "What's your name?" she asked.

"Marcus," he said.

She stumbled momentarily on the coincidence, but recovered—it was only a name, after all.

The boy said, "You will find him, miss, won't you? My mother said you could."

"If I know enough of his variables, I can solve the equation, yes. The equation of where he is. You can help me with that."

"Good," he said, so firmly.

"You like your brother, then?" she asked.

"He's my best friend," the boy said.

As anxious as she was, Seg found herself smiling. Something about the simplicity of the answer, and the cheerful exuberance he stated it with, reminded her unwaveringly of Eck. "I've never had a best friend," she said, "but . . . you remind me of someone I was close to. Her name was Eck."

"Did she die?" the boy asked, and looked up at her with curious eyes. Such a profound thing, death, but he invoked it without any of its weight. Just like Eck would have done.

"No, we just got separated."

"Well, I hope you find her again someday."

"Finally," she said, "someone with some real hope, and without that rotting smell of the barons. Was it you they named this town after?"

"No, I think it was a spring," he said.

Such a literal answer. She then remembered to pull out a little notebook and take some notes.

"Here's as good a place to start as any," she said as they arrived at a large, empty fountain. "If you wouldn't mind getting in and just rolling around a bit."

"Rolling around?"

"Whatever feels right. It will give me an impression of your variables."

As she expected, he took to the task with alacrity, and rolled all over the fountain. Afterward, she took him to other water features of the town, dragged him through an empty ditch, saw how far she could force his arm down a five-centimeter pipe. They even snuck over the fence to the forbidden river, forever in arbitration, and figured out how well he could float. "Very buoyant," she noted, and solved another equation.

She asked him some questions to gauge his mental capacity as well. Even with simple arithmetic he showed himself to be un-schooled, but when she presented the questions as word problems, he proved to be a quick study. At one point she told him, "I'm fairly certain that you'd make a better engineer than Samuel, under the right circumstances. The circumstances are rarely right, though."

Marcus, naturally, didn't mind.

By the end of an entire day of experiments, Seg realized a hard truth—that she still didn't know enough. That she'd never know enough. And she only had one option to proceed. So when she returned Marcus to his mother in the late evening, she said, "I'll need him again tomorrow, first thing in the morning. I'm going to drop him down the same drain. It's the only way."

"No," the mother said. "No, one's already lost—I won't let you lose another."

Seg became so angry that, before she even realized, she'd stricken the mother with her plunger so hard that the woman staggered backward. Already filled with an enormous regret, she followed through and said, "If there's a single thing I can do to save that child, I will do it. And you won't stop me. I'll be here in the morning."

And she walked away.

She arrived, shortly after, at the grave of Plumbess Mar.

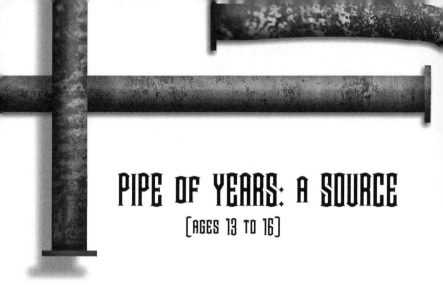

PIPE OF YEARS: A SOURCE
[AGES 13 TO 16]

SEG HAD ALWAYS known that the source of a thing mattered. It mattered for her wood shower, and it mattered for the Orphanage itself, which pulled sparingly—via a long, beautiful aqueduct—from a river several kilometers away. She had revered the plunger as a source of power, and was proven terrifyingly right.

It became increasingly clear to Seg that the Orphanage's main source of orphans was from women who came to give their children away, whether they'd already birthed them or not.

Pregnant women were led to the Top of the Incline. Seg wasn't allowed to go there, but she watched as they arrived, and she watched them leave a week or so later with empty arms. It became an obsession for her, tracking their coming and going.

She spoke to every orphan she could find—words of solace, words of encouragement. She learned their names, their dreams. Her heart broke every time they were deemed incompatible as Plumbesses and passed off to some other family. One thought consoled her, though: at least they'd have a family.

And she continued to wonder—a question that never left her, no matter what Roc said—who her own parents were.

She knew Roc would never tell her. The Plumbess was exceptionally consistent with decisions once she made them. So instead she turned to Zag. Although Zag was very busy, with Eck and with her other duties, she still consistently made time for Seg. Almost every night they spoke, sometimes for hours, in the warm embrace of the valve house.

Seg started with matters at the periphery of her heart—questions about gardening and Plumbing, about what her life might be like as a Plumbess. From there she went deeper, into her annoyance with Eck, her frustration with Roc, and even the fractal trauma caused by the night she flooded the apprentice dormitory and the series of nightmares she'd had ever since. And finally, after seven months of conversations, she broached the subject of her parents.

For seven months Zag had simply listened with the forbearance of a lead pipe. She accepted with equal magnanimity complaints about her ward and her fellow Plumbess, and even shared complaints of her own, transformed somehow into funny anecdotes that always lightened Seg's concern. Delicately she consoled Seg's fear of her plunger. But with the question of her parents, Zag might as well have been Roc.

"Where does the Orphanage water come from?" Zag asked, almost sternly, after Seg had exposed herself so deep.

Unlike Roc, Zag at least had the tendency to ask questions Seg could answer, which she appreciated. "From the Tiber," she replied.

"And before that? Where does it come from before that?"

"Runoff from the mountains, I suppose."

"But is that really where the water comes from? Or is it not precipitated onto the mountains? And before that, isn't it evaporated from all over the world?"

"I know it's a cycle, Plumbess," Seg said.

"But do you think it's the only thing that's a cycle?"

"What do you mean?"

"When you ask where you come from, Seg, and when you're as concerned about it as you are, I'm sure you think you're like a conscientious Plumbess asking where their water comes from. Is it properly sourced, is it fairly sourced? But what I want you to realize is that orphans don't flow to the Orphanage—they evaporate here. And evaporation doesn't care who it takes from. The sun will take from the poor and rich alike. The orphans here are from poor and rich families, the poor who can't afford a child and the rich who are forced from them by circumstance. *The source doesn't matter.* We Plumbesses, old rain clouds that we are, will make sure you get to the right place. We'll deposit you on top of some cold mountain, ready for the next thaw. Only then is it appropriate to talk about what's fair and properly sourced."

After a moment of silence, Seg said, "Roc isn't the best of clouds."

"You'll find that we're all broken in our own way, Seg. All of us here. And although I would've gladly taken you as my apprentice in different circumstances, you would've complained about me, too. Roc will get you where you need to be. And you'll make beautiful rain, Seg."

After that night, Seg didn't ask the question ever again. But she still watched as the women came and went, first with child and then without. Evaporation.

Something inside her was still broken. But at least Zag tried.

PIPE DREAMS
[AGE 16]

THERE CAME A TIME when Seg herself was escorted—no free rein—to the Top of the Incline, to learn the art of birthing babies. It was a skill she'd always wanted, but one part scared her: she would have to do it with a plunger. Although she'd had no further incidents so serious as the flooded dormitory, the damage to her confidence remained. Even in her dreams she turned down any requests for service that required a plunger. She tried to do with her hands what a real Plumbess would never dare, and often failed. Childbirth would be different, she hoped.

Finally at the pinnacle, Seg took a thorough look at the Orphanage and the surrounding land below. No new sights presented themselves, nothing unexpected. Just a slightly different angle on everything she already knew.

"Think you're at the top?" Roc mocked her from behind. "Think you're a Plumbess now? You don't even know the half of it."

Seg didn't respond to the Plumbess's provocation. She'd learned better than that.

Eck came into view, jauntily making her way up the Incline. The wiry girl had her hair pulled back into tight braids. She held her plunger the wrong way, grasped by the head with the handle over her shoulder, but even then she looked like a real Plumbess. Was it the confidence in her bearing? Did Seg look the same?

When Eck reached the Top of the Incline, she didn't bother looking around as Seg had done. Instead, she gave her plunger a flourish and said, "Let's make some babies!"

"Be serious, Eck. This is a grave matter," Seg reproached.

"With you, Seg, everything seems to be," Roc added.

Zag trailed her apprentice by several dozen steps, largely out of breath. The Incline *was* rather steep.

Roc spoke while the other Plumbess caught her breath. "Okay, girls. Remember, today is for observing only. Keep your questions to yourself, I'm not answering them. They'll just be a distraction. Now, are you ready?"

Seg and Eck nodded, Eck more zealously by far. As if in response, a pain-laden cry rose from the building they stood in front of: the Orphanry, where orphans were made.

"Good, sounds like the heifer's ready too. Let's go."

The entrance, the atrium of the Orphanry, didn't have any screaming people in it, just a large stone statue of a Plumbess, a towering figure with a bundled newborn in her right arm and her plunger held maternally before her in her left. Seg recognized her from a book she'd read. "Plumbess Tal," she whispered. The Plumbess who'd founded the Orphanage.

"Yes, yes. Keep moving."

A wing to the left led to a row of rooms. One of the doors stood open, letting out the violent sounds of labor. Roc led the way, and all four entered the room.

Inside, the pregnant woman was on a table, breathing hard and her face flushed red. To her right was a Plumbess, Plumbess Cor, holding her hand and whispering reassuring words. When Cor saw the other Plumbesses, she said, "Oh, good. I wasn't going to wait much longer before doing it myself. She's very progressed."

"I'm here," Zag said. "I'm here. Let me wash my hands, and I'll be right on it." She shuffled over to a sink in the corner, where she took her rubber gloves off and rolled the sleeves of her black shirt up past her elbows.

To the woman, who seemed too locked in her private struggle to care, Plumbess Cor said, "Plumbess Zag will take care of you very soon. Just hang in there."

From where they stood in a corner, as out of the way as they could be, Eck whispered into Seg's ear, "Hey Seg, do you think the birthing canal, do you think it's a supply or a drain? Because the word 'canal' doesn't really have *directionality*, right? What's the frame of reference? Is a child drained from a woman or supplied to the world?"

Fully involved in watching Zag even as the Plumbess simply washed her hands, Seg intended not to answer. But then she considered the question and replied, "It's probably both, Eck."

"Both," Eck said to herself. "Good. Both."

Zag, hands washed, approached the birthing table. The first thing she did was put her ear on the woman's distended belly and listen, which must have been difficult due to the constant vocalizations of pain.

"Breech presentation," she eventually said. "They always seem to be breech. Stand back, please."

Zag did not, as Seg expected, go straight in with the plunger. For half an hour she set it completely aside, speaking to the laboring woman and every once in a while plying with her bare hands. When she finally did take her plunger in hand, the motion she made with it was both simple and profound. It was just a light amount of suction and a small twist, but it produced a baby into the world. The woman, fully drained, collapsed onto her pillow.

"A boy," Zag said, looking at the small, squealing thing in her hands. "Would you wipe him off for me?" she said to Cor, who took the baby from her. Zag then went to wash her hands again.

"Oh, what happens to the boys?" Eck asked, unable to refrain.

"Veal," Roc replied.

"Hmm," Eck said, seeming simultaneously to believe Roc and find satisfaction in the answer.

"Roc," Zag chided from the sink. "Don't lie to the girl, she's very impressionable."

"If she was so impressionable, she'd have remembered I told her no damn questions."

Seg turned her attention to the baby. Plumbess Cor had cut its umbilical cord already, and was getting some towels. Seg kneeled down to it, a small screeching thing whose senses were fighting against a world it didn't comprehend. She said, "You'll never be a Plumbess, little boy. Only lost little girls get the chance. The world is full of little rules like that, so small but so binding. You'll see."

Plumbess Cor was there again, and looked down at Seg. "Would you like to hold him?"

"Yes, please," Seg said. She eagerly extended her arms and the Plumbess settled the baby into them. Seg pointedly never looked at the face of the labored woman, who might as well have been dead to her. She swayed back and forth, humming soft sounds of comfort.

That night, Seg slid into yet another pipe dream, down where nightmares happened and there was no escape. A faceless mother handed her a baby, and she took it into her arms. But then she found that it was heavy, so very heavy that she couldn't move. She looked down and realized that it was lead— still a baby, defenseless and crying, but lead. Thunderstorms were gathering on the horizon, infinite things that crashed lightning and threatened torrents and torrents of rain.

The faceless mother spoke to her. "If you don't move, it will consume you."

"I can't," Seg said, despairing. She couldn't move with the baby, but she would never let go, either. She was trapped, and the storm would hit her. It was a certainty.

The mother's face transformed into that of a snake, and then she bit Seg, right in the embossed memory of her scar. Seg screamed and cradled the baby closer.

She woke to find blood covering her, pooling deeply in the center of her sheets. Terrified, she rushed out the door of her room and down the hall, at that time of night only sparsely lit by candles. She ran to where the Plumbesses slept. They were separated, the Plumbesses and their apprentices, but still close enough to reach in times of need. Seg found the door to Zag's room and knocked frantically.

"Hold on," came the tired voice of the Plumbess.

A few seconds later, the door opened. The room inside was just as dark as the hallway, but Zag still seemed to recognize her. "Is that you, Seg? What's the matter?"

"I had a nightmare," Seg replied. "There was a baby, and a storm."

"Come in, come in," the Plumbess said, and let her through.

Seg took a seat at the foot of Zag's bed, brooding. Already she felt ashamed for having disturbed the Plumbess. She tried to downplay her concern. "Just a pipe dream," she said. "A silly thing."

"Trust your dreams," Zag replied, and sat next to her. She started to settle her arm around Seg's shoulders but startled when she realized Seg was covered in blood.

"What—why is there blood? What happened?"

"It's mine, I think. A snake bit me, in the dream. Or maybe a mother. I'm not sure which."

"You didn't say anything about blood."

"It didn't seem important."

Zag stood back up and Seg could hear her fumbling around in the darkness, looking for towels. "I'll get you cleaned up," she said. "Hold on."

The Plumbess came back and wiped the blood off, but there were no wounds underneath. "Strange," Zag said.

"Is it supposed to rain tomorrow?" Seg asked, lost in her own thoughts. Plumbesses were supposed to be able to tell the weather, but she'd never seen a storm like the one in her dream before.

"No, I don't think so," Zag said. "Not for a week or so."

"Can I stay here tonight, please?"

"Of course, Seg. Of course. Let's finish getting you clean, though."

The next day brought not a storm but a carriage, midnight-black with gold piping. Seg knew it for what it was, though. From as far away as possible—as far up the Incline as she was allowed, on a bench next to a small garden of cabbage—she watched as the smiling demon and the distant storm from her dreams disembarked from the carriage under much pomp and circumstance. Pipe Lords rarely came to the Orphanage, so everyone had gathered to see. Everyone but Seg.

Bent over, she absent-mindedly pulled some weeds as she watched. She was so lost in thought that she nearly screamed when Eck, suddenly appearing beside her, said, "Come on, Seg. There's going to be a feast. Food, Seg! You have to come."

Warily, she joined.

The largest table in the Orphanage was set to the task. The Pipe Lord, Marcus, sat at one end, accompanied by the baron he'd brought along. Next to them were all the Plumbesses of the Orphanage. The apprentices, Seg and Eck among them, sat at the other end of the table. No one else was invited.

The Pipe Lord was saying, " . . . a draining problem, and it's rather serious. I need a solution. I know it's very unusual, my coming here, but I hope a breach in etiquette can be forgiven."

"Unusual," Roc said, for some reason representing the Plumbesses, "but not unwelcome. If it's a draining solution you're looking for, then Eck's your girl. Zag still has nightmares about a hole that girl found in the woods. I'm telling you this in confidence, of course. Zag doesn't like people talking about it."

Zag, annoyed but too polite to argue in front of a Pipe

Lord, simply said, "But of course Eck's not Certified yet, and won't be for some time still."

"If ever," Roc said, and cackled, since that was one of her favorite jokes. Then she yelled down the table, "Well, what do you say, Eck?"

"What?" Eck asked, startled. She'd been staring at the doors to the kitchen, where Plumbess Ark was plunging out the food's final touches. Drool gathered at the corners of her lips.

"Ah, never mind. Hard to make focus, that one. I don't know how Zag puts up with it."

"Easily," Zag said. Then, seeming rather determined to change the subject, she said, "Pipe Lord, didn't Plumbess Sol work at your Manor of Storms, if I'm not mistaken? A very gifted Plumbess."

"Yes, Plumbess Sol, and very gifted indeed," Marcus replied. His tone was bright but his face very grim. "I'm afraid that she spoiled me by showing me everything I could have."

"More than most Pipe Lords could hope for in a lifetime," Zag affirmed.

"Yes . . . but I do have a rather pressing draining problem, as I was saying. Very dangerous."

"Has there been any word from Plumbess Sol?" Zag pressed. "Last I heard, she went on a pilgrimage to the ocean."

"You know more than I do, I'm afraid. She left no notice when she left the Manor. I was half hoping to find her here, so we could pick up where we left off."

"Plumbesses can disappear like that," Roc added, unconcerned. "A rather strange lot, really."

The food was brought out, the wealth of the Orphanage,

the hard labor of so many orphans, steamed and fried and plunged into one magnificent feast. Seg herself didn't have an appetite. For one thing, she involuntarily witnessed Eck swallow a chicken whole—she made sure to look elsewhere for the rest of the meal. But also her thoughts were continuously with the foreboding she'd felt for years, and its strong connection to the man across the table.

Eventually the feast, even among the orderly Plumbesses, dissolved into chaos—hundreds of plates were cleared by a stream of servants, Plumbesses found their wards to give them a few instructions or advice before the night settled in, and the Pipe Lord's baron clamored loudly about a speech he wanted to make.

In the chaos, Seg found Zag so that she might impart a warning. It took a moment for Seg to get her attention—Zag looked just as lost in thought as Seg felt—but eventually she had it. "That man," she said, "is dangerous. He's the one I've been dreaming about. Can you please get him out of here?"

"He's just a man . . . " Zag replied, practically a whisper.

Seg looked over to where the Pipe Lord was standing and was jarred from the conversation. He was talking to Roc and Eck, Roc with her arm maternally over Eck's shoulder and the Pipe Lord laughing amicably. For reasons Seg didn't understand, she left Zag and rushed to intervene.

"Who's this?" she heard Marcus ask as she approached.

"Oh, that one's mine. Seg. Not your girl at all, that one."

"I wouldn't rule anything out," he said, smiling.

"Come on, Eck," Seg said, pushing Roc's arm off and taking the girl by the elbow. "Come on."

Eck resisted, but Seg had always been larger than her, and

she leveraged that advantage. Soon they were out in the hallway, away from the noises of the feast and the beginnings of a speech.

When Seg finally looked into Eck's eyes, she realized she had been too late. The girl was distracted, daydreaming, somewhere else entirely. Somewhere with the Pipe Lord. She slapped her anyway, trying to bring her back around.

Still with a lost look in her eyes, Eck put a hand up to her reddening face. She didn't even hiss, as she might have done if she were truly present. "What was that for?" she asked.

"What did he say to you?" Seg demanded. "Tell me."

"He said . . . he said I reminded him a lot of his last Plumbess. A real Plumbess. And he said he would love to have me work for him when I'm ready."

"You can't work for him," Seg said, trying to keep Eck from drifting away again. "He's evil, he'll destroy you or worse. I've been having nightmares about him for years. You can't—"

"You don't understand, Seg." Eck took on a strange look, like she was seeing Seg for the very first time. She nodded her head, gaining momentum, her voice filled with biting resolution. "Out of all the Plumbesses and apprentices in the room, he said that to me. Not to you, even though everyone looks up to you. To me. And I know what people say about me—I . . . I can't fit in, no matter how hard I try. Raised by snakes, that's what they say about me. I'll always be different. But if someone wants me . . . "

"Oh, you've been mistreated, have you?" Seg countered, anger strangely flaring. "Raised by snakes? At least you had snakes, and now you have Zag. Parents. I've never had anyone." A tear broke out down her face, one she'd done a very good job containing. She turned her back to Eck.

Eck put her hand on Seg's turned shoulder, ever so lightly. Her damaged side. "You have Zag too," Eck replied. "I've seen you talking. Just because you're not her apprentice—that's just a word. Parents . . . that's just another word. I've never told anyone this, but I remember my parents, and I remember their faces. They *gave* me to the snakes, Seg. Most days I try not to think of it, but sometimes I still do. The people who were supposed to love me abandoned me, hoping I would die. They didn't even say goodbye. Is that the kind of memory you're hoping to find?"

If there was an answer, Seg didn't know what it was.

POISONING GRAVES

THE DRY PRINCESS only stayed the one night. Eck stood with the engineer men as the army of desiccated people prepared to leave. Marcus hadn't spoken to her since her insult of the princess the day before.

She was worried, naturally, that someone would discover she'd helped the horses and consider it a crime. She watched nervously as the stablemen handled them, nervously as the dry men harnessed them back up to the carriages. She could've sworn she heard someone say, "These horses look a little too healthy," but it easily could've been her bad conscience.

Marcus departed from the Dry Princess where he'd met her—at the foot of the motionless Fountain. He kissed her hand once but long, and bowed as she looked down at him with amusement. And then she walked down the stairs, straight to the nearest horse.

Eck's breath caught. The moment had arrived—she'd already ruined her appointment as the Plumbess of the Manor of Storms just as she'd ruined every other relationship she was allowed into. The Dry Princess took the horse by the head, looked at it, then called back up the stairs in her whisper of a voice, "Almost, Marcus. Maybe next time." That was all she said before getting back into her palanquin and being carried out the north gate. No alarm was raised, no calls for Eck's immediate removal. Perhaps she was safe.

But watering the horses wasn't her only transgression from the day before. After a day of reflection, she realized she'd insulted the Dry Princess by commenting on her skin. And it felt possible that Marcus would hate her for that, just like Seg had hated her—simply for telling the truth. The Dry Princess really did have terrible skin, like she was in a perpetual state of molting.

Eck approached Marcus with caution in the moments before the first court. "She's a rather unpleasant person, isn't she?"

"Who might that be?" Marcus replied.

"I'm sorry, I meant the Dry Princess."

"Oh, I think she's all right," he replied. His expression was vacant; Eck could tell that his mind was somewhere else.

"She cost us some granaries," Eck replied, trying to bring him back to the matters at hand. The official report on the casualties caused by the Dry Princess's stay had already been given. Three granaries, inexplicably close to the river. Turning off the valves had apparently caused leaks there, and all the food inside was ruined, since it couldn't deal with moisture.

"But the library," he replied, "performed splendidly, from

what I hear. What we need is more solutions like that."

"Not sustainable," she said. "And in this case, not even re-peatable. I only made the library better by teaching it how to use its fountain as a drain, and requesting it to do so. The gra-naries didn't even have fountains, and still they flooded. More drastic measures are needed—the simplest solution would be to let go of the sky or the river. We could make do with just one or the other. There's simply too much wa—"

"No, no," he said, and shook his head vehemently. "That is the one thing we won't do. The Fountain, and the sky and the river connected to it, are the lifework of the last Plumbess. Would you undo the lifework of a fellow Plumbess?"

"If it didn't work right, I absolutely would," she said with her stern voice.

"No. We will not go backward. We will not undo the prog-ress she made. Only forward. I picked you, Eck, because three years ago I was told you could help me with my draining prob-lem. That's why I picked you. I waited all this time for you. Now, did I make a mistake, or didn't I?"

Eck was somewhere between flattered and distraught. Her mind reeled widely until it latched on to what seemed the only path forward. "We'll need a drain to match the magnitude of the Fountain, placed where I see fit. Do you agree to this?"

"Within reason," he said, nodding.

"But that's a long-term solution that will take years to com-plete. In the meantime, I'd like some poisons. The real lethal stuff."

For the first time ever, she smelled fear on Marcus; fear like the breath of a cornered mouse. He said, "What would you need poison for? *Lethal* poison? Why would you have to specify that?"

"It's for the pipes."

He gave her a puzzled look, and she realized she'd have to explain harder than that. "You know, people are just confused, low-quality pipes. And poison, it clears the life right out of them. It's the same principle for better pipes, like the ones you've got around here. Poison will clear them right out."

He looked at her askance for a while, but then nodded his head. "Of course. That makes sense," he said. "The pipes. Yes, I might know a person who can help you." He scanned the court below them, which was about to begin, as if looking for someone. "I'll have a servant take you to him. But afterward—after court."

The bell toned and court convened, which for the morning was a speech from Baron Mason about the benefits of spaying. A few hours after that, Eck was following a servant to the uppermost reaches of the Manor, higher than she'd ever been.

"Must be where you keep the important stuff," she told the servant escorting her.

"No, just Quemar," he replied.

They stopped at a door to a turret. The servant knocked, and a few minutes later, an older man with thinning hair joined them in the hallway. He was quick to close the door behind him, denying a view of the room inside.

"To what do I owe the surprise?" he asked in a low, rattling voice.

The servant spoke for Eck. "I've been instructed by the Pipe Lord to bring the Plumbess to you. She requires poisons."

"Poisons?"

"Don't you have them?" Eck interjected. "He said you did."

"Well of course I have them—it's just rather unusual to be

asked for them. But if it's what the Pipe Lord wants." He took a brief look at the closed door behind him and added, "Just tell me what you need, and I'll have it out for you."

"I don't know what they're called," Eck replied, openly displaying her shame.

"In that case, I'll get you a nice blue lucifer and you can be on your way."

He was already halfway back through his door before Eck could attempt to stop him. "No, not blue lucifer," she said, and grabbed at his wrist.

He maneuvered awkwardly in the doorway to accommodate the changing circumstances. "Well how am I supposed to help you if you don't know what you want, Plumbess?"

"I'll know what I need when I see it," she said firmly.

The man looked at the servant, who shrugged, and then at her again.

"Fine. Fine. But be quick about it."

He allowed her through the door. The servant remained in the hallway.

Inside, the walls were lined with hundreds of strange metal instruments, only a few of which looked like they'd be much use for Plumbing. In the far corner of the room was obviously a human body, although it was mostly disassembled. The man tried to distract her from it by drawing her attention to the other wall, which housed row upon row of glass bottles filled with various liquids and powders. But only Eck could distract Eck.

"Do you kill people in here?" she asked, by way of conversation.

"Why would you . . . what kind of question is that?"

"That's a body over there."

"And I assure you it was already dead when it came into my possession."

"I'm sure it was." Eck meant to display her trust with the statement, but the man didn't seem placated.

"Go ahead, Plumbess, pick your poisons."

With unerring confidence she identified the four that she wanted, after which the man seemed to look at her in a different light. "Good choices," he said. "Very good choices. Well, allow me to get some of each for you. I'm not about to just hand over my whole supply."

"If you will allow it," Eck said, displaying the upper limits of her politeness and pulling a jar from her bag, "I'd like to get what I need myself."

"By all means," he said. "Have at it."

While Eck carefully measured precise amounts from each jar, the man joined the dead body in the corner, which he began noisily trying to shove into a box.

When she was done, she came over and asked him, "What are you doing?"

"Oh, you know, just trying to get this body in a box so it can be disposed of. I'm done with it, for my purposes, so I'd really just like it to go away."

"There's a drain right over there," she said, pointing to a sink next to a complicated set of balances, which appeared to be weighing a large amount of raw fat, probably human.

"I'm aware," he replied.

Remembering to be more specific, Eck rephrased. "Why don't you use your drain to dispose the body?"

The man laughed, although Eck didn't smell any joy in it. Then he said, "If it won't fit in a box, I'm having doubts that it will fit down a drain."

"Would you like me to show you how to use your drain?" she asked.

"Right, that's what I need. Yes, here, show me." He took the severed arm he was holding and forced it into Eck's hands. She was surprised, but received it nonetheless, and took it over to the sink.

Looking down into the sink's bowels, she said, "Maybe it is a bit plugged up." So she traded out the arm in preference of her plunger, and gave the drain a solid strike with the plunger's handle. She nodded in satisfaction, then simply dropped the arm into obscurity.

The man didn't seem to want to believe his eyes. But just like the engineer man before him, his eyes and explanation finally settled on her plunger. "Well of course," he said. "A plunger. But what good is that to me."

"I just cleared your drain up a bit," she said. "It's fine now. You can try it yourself if you don't believe me."

He held up a leg, a good four times thicker than the arm she'd drained. "This, in there? Absolutely not."

"Yes, absolutely yes. All you have to do, when you drop it, is be confident in your heart that you're done with it and want it gone. And have faith that the drain will do that for you. You are done with it, right?"

"Completely used up," he agreed, shaking the leg.

"Then come here and try. Close your eyes. Yes, that's good. And then let go. Completely."

The man did as instructed, and the leg was drained. "That's wonderful!" he exclaimed.

Eck smiled, to show her personality.

"You know, Plumbess, I've decided that I really like you.

A fine taste in poisons, a real practical mind with Plumbing."

Eck's smile turned very quickly into something more genuine. He was the first person to ever say he liked her.

"Wait there, just wait right there—I want to give you something," he said.

He went to consult some cabinets situated over a substantial assortment of knives. After a few moments of scrounging, he came back with a necklace. "May I?" he asked, holding it as if he would place it around her neck.

"Do what?" she asked.

"Put this necklace on you."

"Oh, yes please," she said. "It's very pretty."

"It was my mother's," he said, satisfied as he took a step back to look at it, there where her Lead would have gone— if she were a real Plumbess. "Just loaded with poison. Nightshade."

"Oh, I love it," she said, cupping it in her hands to inspect it closer.

"Now, is there anything else you need?"

"No, that should do it."

"Come along then." He escorted her back to the hallway where he handed her off to the servant. As they walked away, he called after them, "And do come back, Plumbess! A real pleasure."

The servant gave her a strange look as they returned to level ground.

That afternoon, after two weeks of knowing him, Eck learned that the head engineer man had a name—Eric. "One letter away from being a Plumbess name," she told him.

"One letter away, sure, but an entire gender," he replied. "I never did understand why a man couldn't be a Plumbess too. Or a Plumber man, or whatever you want to call it. It never seemed fair."

"I think they told me the reason back at the Orphanage, but I forget what it was."

"How could you forget something so important?"

"Only important to you. I was already appropriately gendered, so it didn't seem to matter."

He was quiet for a while after that. They were walking around the entire Manor—not just the main building, but also the granaries, the stables, the market, and the many peasants' houses that formed the outskirts of the city. By some geographical twist of fate, the Fountain wasn't visible from anywhere a peasant might live, but a single look at one of their drains told Eck that they would feel the consequences of its energy.

She'd spent the entire afternoon in the countryside, gathering every snake she could find. Now, in all the worst drains, she deposited both snakes and poisons. To each snake she said, "Be careful." To each poison she said, "Be deadly."

By the eleventh such drain, Eric broke his silence. "So, I might not be a Plumbess, but poison seems excessive."

"And snakes."

"And snakes."

"It wasn't my first choice," she told him. "I told Marcus that I would rather turn off his river or let loose his sky. But he wouldn't listen to me. I'll find another way, though. I'll do whatever I have to in order to solve the draining problem this city has. I *will* be a successful Plumbess."

"Of course," he said.

They were just about to return to the valve house when a heavy rain began to fall.

"This is never good," Eric said, looking up at the spider web that dominated the sky. "It must be monsooning up there, otherwise water wouldn't make it through. These are always bad—something's going to fail."

"Let's hope for the best," she said.

The best didn't happen. That night, water tore through the city, especially the lower ground, which happened to be where the peasants lived. Three children died. What was worst for Eck was not that she'd failed in making a satisfactory draining solution—the task had just been thrust on her that morning—but that the children didn't die by drowning. It was very clear that they'd died from poisoning, from drainage backflow.

The first court, usually the sole province of idle nobility, was invaded the next morning by an angry mob of peasants. Their spokesperson, a rather vocal old man, declaimed to the Pipe Lord himself, "No disrespect, my lord, but we saw what the Plumbess was doing yesterday. She was pouring chemicals down the drain, chemicals and snakes. Several people saw it. So I ask you to take responsibility for those actions, Pipe Lord. Children are dead."

"What the Plumbess did," Marcus replied, "no doubt saved more lives than you could know, and she did it under my instruction. She was clearing drains—the damage could have been far worse. But furthermore, it is my understanding that the chemicals the Plumbess used were not lethal in their own right—only if your pipes weren't up to code would it have posed a risk. Now I ask you as your liege lord, have you been keeping your pipes up to code, as is your sworn duty? I have a team of engineers ready to perform an inspection, if that is your claim."

For some reason, that settled the matter. The peasants were forcefully removed and the court returned to its usual agenda, which that morning was a speech from Baron Tusk about why cats should be fed four times a day.

Eck was left with the most weighty guilt she'd ever felt. After court was adjourned, Marcus took the time to console her.

"You can't blame yourself for things like this, Plumbess. I've seen far smaller storms do far worse damage. Sometimes people forget that. But to make it up to you, the drain you spoke of yesterday—from now on it's the Manor's top priority. Every resource I have is at your disposal. I have every belief that it will be a marvel to match the Fountain itself, with you guiding it."

The flattery, and the hope of a real drain, lightened Eck's guilt, but only a little. "The children, will they be buried with your father?"

It was a question he wasn't expecting. "Well, not really *with* my father, there will be the proper amount of separation, but they'll be buried in the Manor's graveyard, yes. I allow the peasants that."

"Will you tell me where it is?"

"I'll have my servant—"

"Will *you* tell me where it is?"

"Of course, Plumbess."

That afternoon, Eck watched the burial of three children. She sat among the trees, at an awkward distance from the mourning crowd. Her presence didn't go unnoticed.

The old man from before shouted, "That's her right there,

the one responsible! The audacity, the audacity! Pipes to code! *Pipes to code!?* "

A woman, equally old but much softer, took him by the elbow and led him back to the graves, where the funeral rites continued.

Eventually, they dispersed, but Eck did not. She stayed sitting there until late in the evening, until a familiar voice startled her.

"Plumbess, I didn't expect to find you here. What are you doing?"

It was the poison man, Quemar. He had a brutal shovel over his shoulder, like he was about to do some serious gardening.

"I killed them," she said, gesturing to the new graves. "With the poisons you gave me."

"Now, I wouldn't," he stammered, "wouldn't phrase it like that, no. Accidents, Plumbess. Natural causes. Coincidences. Twists of fate."

"What are you doing here?" Eck asked, preferring not to dwell on the topic of her failure after admitting it clearly the once.

"Oh, I'm here, if you really want to know, to dig up the bodies."

"Isn't that disrespectful?" She didn't know much about graveyards, but she imagined people were buried for a reason.

"Disrespectful," he said slowly, tasting the word. "It is, yes, I think it very much is. But listen to this. I can very much use these bodies. The way they are now, just sitting there, they aren't very much use. So I ask you what's wrong and what's right."

"You're probably right," she admitted.

That brightened his face. He said, "If I might be so bold, Plumbess, would you like to help me? There's nothing like manual labor to take the mind off things, I do believe. And I brought two shovels." He rotated slightly to give her a view of the second.

"Why would you bring two?" she asked.

"Sometimes I lose the first one. Now what do you say?"

She thought about it for just a moment, but then agreed. She took his extra shovel, and as he went to work on the nearest grave, she took the one right next to it.

As he had claimed, the work really did clear her mind. It transported her to a better time, to gardening on the Incline and emptying septic tanks with Seg. For several hours she was lost in the simple act of stabbing and lifting, stabbing and lifting. The digging wasn't especially hard—the graves were fresh, after all—and before she knew it she was waist-deep in a hole of her own making. Then a morbid thought struck her: if she dug any farther, there was the chance that she herself would strike upon the body.

"Do you mind," she asked, "if I start on the last one and you finish this one?"

"Not at all, Plumbess."

And so she did—she repeated the process, lost in the mechanical motions, until a latent dread stopped her again from going any farther. Then she climbed out and waited, as there was nothing else for her to do.

Soon, Quemar had completely uncovered the first of the graves and dragged a boy—a corpse wrapped in linen—out. Eck wouldn't look at the body, but she did look at the hole it left behind.

"It's so deep," she said, standing at the edge.

"Not really," he replied, but after he saw her expression he looked again, probably suspecting she meant something different.

"How many of these graves are empty?"

He shielded his eyes with his hand, as if blocking out the moonlight, and surveyed around him. "Every body in the past six years. Now that you mention it, I've probably cleared out this entire half of the graveyard. Yes, that sounds right."

"Do you mind," she asked, "if I go and get some things?"

"You have to stop asking me for permission all the time, Plumbess," he replied. "You're the one doing me a favor."

"Oh, right. Well, I'll be right back."

In the darkness, she made her way around to the valve house. She'd made the trip at night before, so this time she performed it with ease. Once there, she turned to a stack of piping materials that the engineer men kept there for maintenance activities. She took everything she could carry in her arms and returned to the graveyard, where she dropped them down into the first empty grave.

As she lowered herself down after them, Quemar walked up and asked, "May I now ask what *you're* doing, Plumbess?"

"It's like you said," she replied. "About the bodies—that they can be useful. These empty graves, they can be useful too. I just need to route a few pipes, and they can act as weeping tiles—like a drain, for the ground. There's no point letting all these graves sit around useless. They *are* very deep."

"Yes, they are," he agreed, as if finally seeing the same thing. "Well, I'll be right over here if you need me."

As the dawn finally arrived—Quemar had long since left,

after shaking his head in awe and hoisting three children's bodies onto his shoulders—Eck completed her work. With bare hands she shook the dirt from her hair. She'd completely worked through her gloves.

The result was a network of pipes that rivalled the one in the sky. Instead of catching clouds, it brought together the former resting places of an entire city. As impressive as it was, it was completely hidden. Only a few inconspicuous drains peeked out, flush with overgrown gravestones and the occasional bush.

With her work, she left Dennis. "Make sure it drains," she told the viper. "No poison this time. Just weeping tiles and you."

THE LEAD

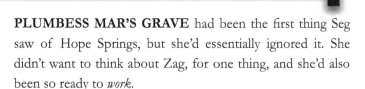

PLUMBESS MAR'S GRAVE had been the first thing Seg saw of Hope Springs, but she'd essentially ignored it. She didn't want to think about Zag, for one thing, and she'd also been so ready to *work*.

Her situation had changed. Now, she needed to understand a drain, a drain designed by another Plumbess. And that required understanding the Plumbess herself.

Like before, the place was deserted. It didn't surprise Seg. If hardly anyone in the town knew what a Plumbess was, they surely wouldn't pay tribute to one. She sat at the foot of the statue and unfolded the blueprint of the drain. In the final light of the day, she studied it hard and thought about all the things she knew.

It was almost completely dark when the clearing of a throat startled Seg back to reality. "Who is it?" she asked, jumping to her feet and holding her plunger, ready to attack.

When she saw that it was Baron Seth, looking a little worse for wear, she didn't lower her plunger.

"What are you doing here?" she asked.

"The trial," he said. "It's been reminding me of Mar. I came here to visit her."

"To visit her? You make it sound like you got along."

"She was one of the best people I ever knew," he said, and appeared broken by the admission.

"Then why are you keeping your river from her?"

That sent him sputtering. "I, I'd never . . . I may have represented it differently in court, as I'm sure you can understand, but I would've trusted everything I own to Mar. But not these fools she left behind—not Carral or Gregor or any of the rest."

Seg bent over to pick up the blueprint of the drain, which she studied for one final moment before folding it up and returning it to her pocket. Then she unfolded the blueprint she really knew, the one centered around a river. The supply. She spread it out on the ground.

She said, "It's a cycle. Plumbess Mar taught everything she knew, everything she *was*, to Plumbess Zag, and Plumbess Zag . . . she did the same for me. I *am* Plumbess Mar. And if you trusted me with your river once, you should trust me with it again."

On a lighter note she added, tracing the river's white course with her finger, "I think you've overstated its size. I've looked over your fence."

"It used to be bigger," he complained. Then, bending down to get a better look, he said, "These are the plans Mar made?"

"Half of them," Seg answered. "It seems like she started with building the drain system first, as any sensible person would. She never got around to building any of this. But I could. I would have to make some changes—things have changed—but I could finish what she started. After . . . after I save this boy."

The baron slowly began to nod. "Yes," he said. "Yes. My river, I'll . . . give it to you. Not to the barons, not to the Pipe Lord. I won't let this river be just another thing for them to attach a hose to and pretend it's a, a *benediction*. No, I'll give my river to you and you alone."

After a month of listening to the baron fight like a cornered animal against even the slightest of concessions, Seg couldn't believe what she was hearing. But she wasn't about to let such an opportunity pass her by. She took her pen and, in the empty corner of the blueprint, wrote out a short Contract of Work, which she was legally disposed to do since Carral had never bothered.

"If you mean it," she said, "you'll sign this."

The baron took her pen and looked at it for far longer than he looked at the contract itself. "Yes," he said again. "You have a deal." He was talking, Seg noticed, to the statue.

In the wake of that surreal moment, Seg returned to her hovel. She knew that, as tired as she was, a night of sleep would do her more good than any other preparation. Her sleep, however, was not restful. In her mind she was already lost in the drain, drowning in water she couldn't even see. She woke to find her Lead caught in the splintered edge of her bedframe, pulling the chain tightly across her throat. To escape, she rolled off her bed. She didn't sleep anymore after that.

Instead, she packed a few things into her bag—the blueprint, some carrots, a candle. Then she waited for the sun to rise before setting off to get Marcus.

When the mother answered the door, Seg felt another sharp pang of remorse. The whole left side of her face was bruised. Even worse, the woman had become painfully eager to please Seg. "Good to see you, miss. Yes, I'll get him right away. He's sleeping still, but I'll wake him up. Is there anything else you need, miss?"

There was one thing. In a softer tone than she'd ever used before, although the damage was already done, Seg asked, "Does Eric have any extra clothes that Marcus could wear? The closer we can get to mimicking the exact conditions of the fall, the better."

"He only has the one pair of pants, the pair he's wearing," the mother replied. "But he does have a second shirt. I'll have Marcus wear the shirt, yes. Right away, miss."

Soon, the boy was produced, looking natural in his brother's shirt. That was encouraging for Seg. "Let's go," she told him, and together they made their way to the cavernous drain.

"It's a dangerous thing we're doing," she told him. "I want that to be perfectly clear."

"We'll be fine," the boy responded with a slight smile and an undue amount of confidence. "We'll find him, I'm sure of it."

The Plumbess and the boy struggled in no way with the boards that barred the cavern. The morning light struck the drain differently than it had the afternoon before. Seg made a final note on a piece of paper that she then returned to her bag.

Marcus stood at the foreboding edge of the drain. Fear entered his delicate features as he looked down.

"Do you love your brother?" Seg asked.

"Yes," he said, a firm resolve.

"I'm sorry," she said, and pushed him over the edge.

With everything Seg knew, with all the time she'd spent looking over blueprints and solving equations, still she couldn't reach the answer. Only a falling boy could do that for her. A surprised, falling boy. And the look on Marcus's face was sheer surprise as firm ground left him. Surprise and the sudden fissures of a fractured trust as his eyes briefly caught Seg's. Eric, too, would have been surprised as he fell, and every variable counted.

She jumped in after him. Like a ragdoll, he bounded off the walls, taking some especially hard hits when the piping suddenly turned. Where he turned, Seg used her plunger to follow him. The first left he took she was confident about, having solved it. But she nearly lost him when he, against all odds, fell through a small offshoot in one of the longer, wider stretches. Still, she managed, and after another few minutes of plummeting, they finally came to a stop.

Seg tried immediately to fix what she had broken. "Are you all right?" she asked the boy.

He obviously wasn't—his forehead was split open and his right arm appeared to be broken. He tried to repress it, but the pain—or disappointment—forced a single tear out of his right eye. "I'm fine," he said.

Seg was damaged herself, this time, but ignored it. "I'm sorry. I had to do it, to find your brother. If you come over here, I can do something about your cut."

"I said I'm fine. Find my brother."

"You have to lead," she said. "That's why you're here."

He didn't argue, or say a word at all. He simply limped forward into the darkness.

Seg had her candle, but wouldn't light it. Eric, too, would have stumbled around in darkness, looking for a way out. So many variables. She traced her hand along the pipe and felt its cold corrosion. Again it amazed her how much damage forty years could do. Plumbess Mar. She thought about her chance encounter with Baron Seth, about the Contract of Work folded at her breast. She felt the strings of fate tighten around her again and weigh her down. She took her Lead in her hands to keep it from pounding against her heart.

At the first branch they reached, Marcus yelled, "Eric!" and then waited silently for an answer.

"Don't yell his name," Seg said. "Yell your own."

Although they weren't on good terms, and although he obviously felt foolish doing it, the boy took her advice. "Marcus!" he yelled. And even though no sound returned, he seemed convinced by the left branch, and limped forward.

Several hours of ponderous wandering went by, and then he asked, "How deep are we? How far do these pipes go? None of this seems possible." His voice quaked a little, his natural buoyancy failing him.

"Drains . . . real drains, like this one, can't really be expressed by depth or length. They don't really have direction, either. They just go where they need to." Underneath the thin layer of everything she knew, all the theory and magic, Seg was terrified herself. Her knuckles around her plunger were so white that they glowed, but otherwise she kept a good façade.

She said, "Still, they can be navigated if you have faith. That's what they respond best to—a faith in what they can do. So believe in finding your brother, Marcus."

This inspired him to take a few more steps, but then he stopped. "What's this?" he asked.

It was so dark that Seg had to step forward to answer him. Her hands, held out before her, touched cold steel, sheered, bent out of its natural shape and folded in on itself, blocking the pipe ahead of them. "An Obstruction," she whispered. It was the only path forward, and it was blocked. "We must have . . . taken a wrong turn somewhere. He can't have gone this way. Let's . . . let's go back."

Her situation was more dire than she could admit. If they'd taken the wrong turn, then it was unlikely they'd ever find the right path. She'd lost the boy. Even prepared, as prepared as she could be in such an emergency, she'd failed. She'd put the entire effort of her being into it and had found only an Obstruction.

Her fear poured out of her, and the drain dilated to receive it. She was on the very edge of running away when the boy said, "But . . . but I swear I can feel him on the other side."

"You . . . are you sure?" she asked. It was a stupid question, but she wasn't fully composed yet. She tried to regather.

"No," he said, finally falling into full despair. Her fear had washed over him. "We're lost, aren't we? Marcus . . . "

"Trust your intuition," she said, firmer. "And go stand back there. If I . . . if I clear this, then it's possible we'll all drain out, even your brother."

She waited until his footsteps sounded distant. Then she took her plunger and struck the Obstruction with all the feeling she could manage. Nothing happened. Such a large Obstruction, in a drain she didn't understand.

"Only anger can remove an Obstruction," she whispered. The only anger she could find was at herself, anger for not knowing more about drains. If Eck were there, she could've easily found the child without endangering the life of another one. If Seg were a *real* Plumbess, she could've saved Zag. She struck the Obstruction again, and darkness exploded around her.

Suddenly very afraid, she frantically tried to find the candle in her bag, but just as her hand clasped around it she was siphoned away, through so much darkness and into—a corridor.

It was nowhere she'd seen before, sparsely lit by torches. Wherever she was, she hoped the boy was all right—he wasn't there with her.

She picked up her plunger off the ground, where she'd dropped it in preference of the candle. Then she walked down the corridor. An alcove slowly exposed itself on the left. In its center was a statue standing in front of a coffin, both made of stone. Everything was as still as death itself—even the torch that she now stood in front of cast no lively shadow.

She recognized the Plumbess—a stern figure holding a child bundled in her arms. Plumbess Tal, the Plumbess who had founded the Orphanage. There was an identical statue in the Orphanry.

At the Plumbess's feet was a plaque, but it was completely defaced. No name, no date, no epitaph—no recounting of her grand achievements. Nothing. Seg moved on.

Every third torch there was another coffin and a statue of a Plumbess. Some she recognized, most she didn't. None of the plaques had names, and some of the statues even lacked faces—just humanoid stone holding the imitation of a plunger. The corridor always bent slightly to the right; Seg had the distinct impression that it was just one large circle, and that eventually she'd find Plumbess Tal again, having gotten nowhere.

But then she came upon Zag, which dissipated all thoughts of progress.

Seg looked down, down on the Plumbess who had meant everything to her. Even in stone, her face was soft. It was much different than the statue in Seg's dreams—*that* Zag had been enormous, unreachable. This one . . .

The plaque, like all others, was defaced. "No," she said. "No, Zag. You will have a name."

From her bag she took a screwdriver, and got to her knees. She made the stroke that would have been the top line of a *z*, but upon impact, the screwdriver, and her hand with it, became stone.

"Agh!" she screamed. She tried pulling away, but she was stuck. The stone held her, the stone *was* her, slowly moving up her wrist and into her forearm. Panicking, she struck at the plaque with her plunger, but nothing happened. So she did the only thing left to her—she struck her own arm off, right at the elbow, and crumpled to the floor.

For a while she just lay there, gathering herself. The stump of her arm seemed stable—a clean break. "Just a pipe dream," she told herself. "Just a pipe dream."

She was then lifted, by the neck, to her feet. And the face that came into view—where the statue of Zag should have been—was Eck. Although she moved, she too was stone. Her face was a lifeless smile, and she looked down on Seg as her hand constricted around her neck.

"How . . . " Seg gasped. "You're . . . you're not dead. Why are you here?"

The statue wouldn't answer. The pressure around Seg's neck grew until she couldn't breathe. Her eyes frantically searched the corridor for help, but no one came. Zag was gone. She was alone.

She tried using her plunger. She struck at Eck like she'd done months before, but it wasn't the right hand—the strikes were weak, useless.

Then she realized that it wasn't Eck's hand, but her own necklace that was suffocating her—her Lead. And only then did she realize just how *literal* it was. For months it had done nothing but weigh her down; nothing but make it hard for her to hold her head up. It even choked her in her sleep like it was surely choking her now. And it would, if she let it, keep her from accomplishing her first real task as a Plumbess—saving a child.

But its weight went back farther than just a few months— its poison leached through time, through all her memories and everything she knew and was, all the way to the beginning. For the first time she looked at it clearly, at the damage it had caused.

For years she'd convinced herself that because she was an orphan, she was alone. And so she felt alone. And Roc, as much as Seg had always hated her, told her the one thing she needed to hear when it mattered most—that she couldn't hate Eck. Eck had only told Seg the truth. Seg couldn't have saved Zag. She hadn't been ready.

And Eck—the real Eck, not this stone imitation—had always been there for Seg, when Plumbing was hard, when her loneliness was overwhelming, when the very waves of her dreams crashed down on her.

The loss of Zag was a weight Seg would always carry, but she didn't have to wear it around her neck. So she calmly exhaled the very last of her breath, took her plunger firmly in hand, and struck the only thing holding her back: the real Obstruction. She struck the Lead.

PIPE OF YEARS: SEPTIC
[AGES 16 TO 19]

SEG DELIVERED MORE babies than any apprentice ever had. In an unhealthy way, it helped her. In her mind, she was liberating innocent children from women who didn't love them. As unfortunate as their circumstances were, at least they'd start life in hands that cared about them: her own.

She got the feeling that the other Plumbesses knew why she spent so much time at the Orphanry—they always seemed to *know*—but none of them criticized her motives. Roc even encouraged her, since she was using her plunger again and finding comfort in its terrible power. She even started helping people in her dreams again, after years of refraining.

There was another reason she liked the Orphanry—Eck was rarely there. Eck didn't have the same aptitude for delivering babies that Seg did, or the same need for escape, or whatever it was. When she was there, she spent a majority of the time explaining to pregnant women that they should have laid their eggs instead, and then delving into the benefits. She didn't convince any of them.

She didn't convince Seg either. Seg became a messiah of

birth; she practiced and practiced until she was better than any Plumbess she knew. Even Roc, who she'd never before impressed, complimented her skill.

At the same time, her apprenticeship was reaching its inevitable end. There was no infinite Incline. The last topic, supposedly the most difficult, was septic systems. They seemed simple enough—human waste flowed into a large tank, where it sifted into three layers: a solid layer at the bottom, a water layer in the middle, and a scum layer at the top. Bacteria worked on the waste during its residence there, breaking down organic material until it was harmless. Then, relatively clean water would flow out of the tank into the leach field where it was slowly introduced, through perforated pipes, back into the world. After enough solid waste built up, it could be removed as compost. Simple enough.

But the minutia of septic systems were very important, and hard to control—the type of bacteria, the type of waste likely to enter the system, the topography of the region, the size of the perforated holes, the porosity of the soil in the leach field, and so much more. If even one variable was wrong, untreated waste could enter the water supply.

As part of the learning process, Seg and Eck had to shovel the composted remains of a stale septic tank. It reminded Seg of being a child again, of digging outhouses. The distinction between outhouse and septic system seemed small, and the time between flattened to a moment. But Seg didn't mind. It was better than the broken leach field she'd had to fix a few weeks before, which had smelled like raw death. The sulfur smells of that forsaken place didn't leave her for weeks, and she felt compelled to avoid the Orphanry for just as long out of fear and respect.

Eck seemed to enjoy the digging. "This is how everything should be."

Seg couldn't help but ask. "What do you mean?"

"If you smell, if you need purifying, you should spend a few years underground until you're ready again."

"You're welcome to try," Seg said, and scraped the bottom of the tank with her shovel.

"But I don't smell. I was thinking of Plumbess Tes. She should be buried somewhere for a while. Or burned. Yes, I think burning might accomplish the same thing. After the initial smoke, of course."

Plumbess Tes was the oldest Plumbess in the Orphanage, and, as Eck had blithely condemned, was rather on the decaying side of life. "You shouldn't talk about burning Plumbesses like that," Seg replied. "No matter how much they smell."

"I promise that even when you're a Plumbess, Seg, I'll tell you when you smell." She smiled, and threw a load of human waste over her shoulder. "I'll even help you fix it, if you let me. If you don't want to be burned or buried, we can find something else."

GREYWATER

[AGE 19]

ALTHOUGH THE ORPHANRY was at the highest point of the Incline, it was not at the center of the concentric circles that formed the Orphanage. Instead, there was a circular pit with sheer walls five meters or so in height. When it was time for the final test, the only test standing between Seg and her Certification, Roc and Zag brought her there—to the only part of the Orphanage she'd never seen.

It was a strange place. Pipes lined the entire circumference of the wall, which itself wasn't strange—the Orphanage was practically built out of pipes. What was strange was what they were made out of: lead. And at the end of every lead pipe was a pipegram. As Seg and Eck stood there, other Plumbesses came and went, receiving and sending messages.

"Are we going to learn to use those?" Eck asked, looking at the pipegrams with a strange avarice.

"No, girl. The entire time you're here, you're not to touch any of the valves. Under no circumstances. Understood?"

Eck and Seg both nodded.

Seg asked, "Then why *are* we here?"

"It's like this," Zag said. "You've got to show us everything you've learned. All the concepts, all the skills. And that will take time. You'll be here for a month. You'll eat here, sleep here, live here. And you can't leave."

Zag gestured to an enclosure in the center of the pit, a short, white fence that defined a circle with a twenty-meter diameter. Another fence divided it into two halves, and Seg felt the sinking certainty that she'd be spending an entire month with Eck.

"You'll be given eighty liters of water, and only eighty liters of water. Some of it you'll drink. All of the food you eat, you'll have to grow yourself—we've given you a whole assortment of seeds, and we've even got some squash already growing for you. No other food will be given to you. So far, you might think that sounds easy enough—just some gardening, and you've done plenty of that. But there are more conditions. Every night, a Plumbess will come by and smell you. You must smell decent enough for society,"—Eck smiled—"and that means you might have to wash your clothes every now and then. The sun won't be kind."

The ceiling of the pit was nonexistent, perfectly exposing the enclosure to the sky.

Zag continued, "There will also be two women who will come to each of you sometime during the month with babies for you to deliver. You'll want to wash your hands for that, among other things. In short, you'll have to *live* for a month, and do all the things that living people have to do. I think you'll find the test rather difficult. You'll be up against some real constraints—constraints like you've never seen before. When you're a Plumbess, you'll work for a Pipe Lord. And, born in privilege, they won't understand constraints. They'll ask you to build pipes for the most trivial things. They'll ask you to waste water as if resources were infinite, as if it weren't a matter of life and death.

"You will have to be a balance to them—that is your duty. And, being an orphan, you will inherently understand privations and constraints in a way they never will. But I hope you'll also realize that, as much as you know and are, you're not much better than these men of privilege. You are still a desiring, wanting being. You'll have to fight even yourself. This next month will prepare you for that. Now, are you ready?"

"Will Seg and I be allowed to talk to each other?" Eck asked, looking at the short fences.

"No, Eck, that would be cheating," Seg replied.

"Yes, you can talk to each other. Knowing you two, I imagine that your approach to the problem will be very different—really, I wish you *would* learn from each other, but I doubt there's any likelihood of that. But if that's the only question you have, then let's get started."

Seg entered her side of the enclosure. It was a simple, barren place. There was a single cot in the middle, with a single set of sheets. Squash, as promised, grew along the edge, right next to an outhouse—an *outhouse*, of all things. She'd also been given a large assortment of books, and an even larger assortment of tools and building materials. Her water, all eighty liters of it, was in a steel tank about half a meter in each dimension. It had a spigot on its bottom. That was everything.

The first big project she would undertake was a bit of gardening. If she hoped to eat, then the seeds would have to be buried immediately, as the squash would only hold her over for a little while. Even with the use of a plunger, it would be a week before she could produce anything. And it would take a lot of water.

She started with reading, to see if she could figure out which plants had the best ratio of nourishment to water expenditure. It was a thing she'd never considered before. After several books and much deliberation, she picked a small variety of potatoes and a couple of fruits, and planted those.

The only thing that would make her eighty liters of water last a whole month was an efficiency technique called greywater: the water she used for washing her clothes and hands could be collected in a bucket and then used to water her plants. But greywater would only get her so far.

So, after five solid days of gardening, she moved on to her next large project—an improvement on her outhouse. As it was, the outhouse was very wasteful. Even if she was able to create a septic system and get good use out of it in less than a month, though, would she want to use its product as fertilizer? At least she didn't have to commit to an answer just yet—she could build now and think later. So she dug some more holes, welded some pipes, and made some Plumbing.

The decision of what to do with her own urine was harder. She could urinate directly on her plants—but would she want to eat them afterward, the potatoes especially? Was there something she could do to filter it, to make it more acceptable in her mind? It still seemed inappropriate to her, like the water that came out of her was fatally tainted. But after nearly a week of eating only squash, her mind wandered to strange places, and she even considered what it would take to make her urine potable. Fortunately, the thought left her.

Every night, a Plumbess came to smell her. Early on, she moved her cot as far away from the outhouse as possible to improve her odds—she didn't need some errant odor influencing the Plumbess's opinion. And she used about a handful of water each time to scrub out the most offending of stains, which she individually smelled and sorted. She had, after all, a lot of time.

And although she saw the occasional nostril flare, the Plumbesses who smelled her never said one way or the other what they thought. They just came and went, which was enough to give Seg anxiety. She spent whole afternoons in anticipation and evenings in regret.

It was on the eighth day that the first unborn child was brought to her.

"Let me . . . let me wash my hands," Seg told the escorting Plumbess, after eight days of saying nothing. "Take her to the cot. I'll be right over."

She went to her tap of water and washed her hands. She used more water than she should have, but at least she caught the waste with a bucket. Food for the plants, she thought.

As usual, she said nothing to the laboring woman, neither to reassure nor to explain. She simply did what she did best— she delivered a baby, a little girl. She took the girl to the water tap for a slight rinsing, and again used more water than she should have. "More food for the plants," she told the little girl.

She then handed the baby over to the Plumbess and watched as they left.

The cot, unfortunately, was stained from the event. Rather than wash it, which would have taken a very large amount of water, she elected to spend every night after that on the ground.

The time went slowly, painstakingly, by. Unlike all the other tests, she couldn't lose herself in the work, couldn't distract herself from the larger questions that haunted her. There was too much time, and to constantly work would be wasteful. So, she thought a lot.

It was already the eleventh day, and the potatoes were blooming, when she remembered again that Eck was just across the fence. She hadn't heard a word from her.

She looked over the fence to see what her lifelong neighbor was up to. She was amazed by what she saw. The contrast to Seg's own enclosure couldn't have been starker. Seg's half was an industrial spectacle—Eck's was a wasteland. It took Seg a few moments to realize that the motionless bundle lying on the cot was, in fact, Eck.

"Eck, what are you doing?" Seg asked. "When you asked Zag if we could talk, I was worried I'd never hear the end of you."

Eck rolled over, and the face she presented was gaunt and sickly pale. Still, she smiled at the sight of Seg. "Seg . . . Seg, good to see you."

"Eck, you look horrible. Are . . . are you okay? Are you sick? If you told a Plumbess, I'm sure they would—"

"No," Eck rasped. "Not sick. It's my . . . it's my plan. I've been sleeping, mostly. I don't think I've had any water yet. How are my squashes? I can't see them from here."

The squash, a few paces away, were dried to a husk.

"Eck," Seg said, managing to find concern, "that's insane. The whole point of this is to *live* for a month. What you're doing isn't living."

"Some people live like this," Eck replied.

"What about your smell?"

"I don't smell," she said, and gave another thin smile. "Just . . . just like a rock doesn't smell."

"And delivering babies? What about that?"

"I've already done one," Eck replied.

"I don't believe you."

"I didn't do anything, if that's what you mean. Babies can pretty much birth themselves, so I just let it do that."

"And the Plumbess just let you do that?" Seg was now indignant. She'd used so much water on that child.

"She didn't say anything."

Seg couldn't stop shaking her head. "Well, you can't kill yourself, Eck."

"I won't."

Eck's reassurance, and her judgment in general, didn't reassure Seg. But Plumbesses did come by and look in at them every now and then, whenever they had a message to send. Hopefully they wouldn't let Eck kill herself. It was a very stupid way to solve the problem, Seg thought. For her own part, she returned to gardening.

On the sixteenth day, there was a large commotion of Plumbesses in the pit. Seg set aside her septic efforts to figure out what was going on, but no one would answer her calls for information.

Later that afternoon, she heard Zag talking to Eck. "I'll be back before your thirty days are up," she said. "I just have to take care of this real quick."

By the time Seg made it to the fence to see what was going on, the Plumbess was already gone. She asked Eck where Zag had gone, but Eck just shrugged.

Seg did, in the end, everything she could—everything she had to do to make her water last. She built, she conserved, she reused. She made some of the hardest decisions she'd ever made with her own urine. She lived off of squash, potatoes, and the occasional berry. But it wasn't enough.

In the beginning she thought it would be thirst, if anything, that would break her. But on the nineteenth day, the second unborn child was brought into her enclosure, and she didn't have enough water to properly wash her hands.

To the Plumbess who brought her, Seg said, "Take her to the Orphanry. Take her . . . somewhere else."

"Excuse me?" the Plumbess said.

"Take her somewhere else!" Seg yelled, defiant in her shame.

More than anything, she wanted to be a Plumbess. But she would not, under any circumstances, endanger a child.

"But you have to deliver the baby."

"I'll talk to Roc about that," Seg said, and left her enclosure.

She found Roc in the Middle of the Incline, directing some servants as they stacked up sandbags. The Plumbess looked surprised to see her, but not too surprised. "What are you doing here?" Roc asked.

"I ran out of water," Seg said, simply. "There was a baby I had to deliver, but I couldn't wash my hands."

"So you gave up?"

Seg just nodded. She didn't want to vocalize her failure.

Roc looked off to the horizon. At what, Seg didn't know. "That makes sense, I suppose."

"You're not mad?" Seg asked.

"No, I'm not. In fact, you're going to be the one mad at me when I tell you, but the test wasn't meant to be passed."

"What?"

"It's just supposed to be a lesson. A lesson that you can try as hard as you want, learn everything we have to teach you, care as much as possible, and make all the right ethical choices, but in the end, you will still waste. Because you're a human. But nineteen days—yes, I've been keeping track of you, I've been watching, and I must say that I'm . . . I'm proud of you, Seg. You did well."

Seg didn't know how to respond.

"As a reward," Roc said, "would you like to hear the last secret the Orphanage has to offer you?"

Seg just nodded, and Roc led her back up to the Incline, back into the pit where she'd spent the last few weeks.

"If it really is impossible," Seg said, "then someone should tell Eck. Because she'll either succeed anyway or die in the process. Have you seen the way she looks?"

"That's between Eck and Zag," Roc replied.

"But is Zag even here? I heard her say a few days ago—"

"And," Roc said, interrupting her, "Eck can take care of herself. Now do you want to hear what I have to tell you or don't you?"

"Yes," Seg said.

Roc took her to the wall of piping, the one she'd been told under no circumstance to touch. "This room," Roc said, stroking one of the lead pipes as if she might love it, "is called the Sump."

"The Sump?"

"And the reason you've never been told about it is that a naïve little girl like yourself would be sorely tempted by its power. It is, I assure you, the finest work of Plumbing in the entire world. Each of these lead pipes goes to a different town or city, as you might guess. But it's not only for sending messages with the pipegrams.

"It's called the Sump because, in times of urgency—floods, natural disasters, and bad Plumbing—it can be used to help drain the city on the other side. But it's very complicated, and very dangerous. Because it's lead, its misuse could poison both the land and the people of the Orphanage. Only a Plumbess who understands lead can avoid that. And even then, the sheer amount of water could destroy this place. I'm telling you all this not so you can use it. You still don't know much about the world, and you certainly don't understand lead. I'm telling you because if you're ever in real trouble—remember what a single dream can do, girl, remember that dormitory you flooded—you can call on the Orphanage and we can help you. Remember that."

"I will," Seg replied. She was not, however, as sorely tempted as Roc seemed to assume. She was more worried, for whatever reason, about Eck. "Listen, Roc, can I talk to Eck? Just to make sure she's okay?"

Roc smiled. "Yes, girl. On one condition—don't tell her what you know about the test being futile, or about the Sump. She'll find out on her own, when the time is right."

"Fine," Seg said, and walked over to the fenced enclosure.

The contrast between their two approaches had grown starker. Eck's half now looked like a sunned sickroom, covered in spider webs and dust. "Eck, are you alive?"

"Seg? What are you . . . doing here?"

"I gave up."

Eck took a long, feeble time to think about that. "Will you still be a Plumbess?' she finally asked.

"I don't know."

"Well I hope you will. I . . . I drank some water yesterday."

"That's good, Eck. That's what people do."

Reassured enough, Seg left her there, but she visited her again the next day, and the day after that.

That was when it started to rain. "See? You should've held out just a little longer," Eck told her when she visited shortly after.

Eck sat up for the occasion, and even stood. She managed a few stumbling steps to her water tank, where she indulged in a few drops. Then she surveyed her enclosure for what might have been the first time.

"My squashes!" she exclaimed. "When did that happen?"

"They needed to be watered, Eck," Seg said. "You know that."

Seg was jealous on account of the sudden rain, but Eck soon made it clear that she didn't know how to make use of the windfall.

"How do you collect rain?" she asked. "I bet it could be useful."

"How do you collect rain? Are you sure you're ready to be a Plumbess?" Seg replied.

"Fine, don't tell me," she said, and went to get her sheets. She spread them out on the ground, perhaps thinking it would hold the rain for her. Seg left her to her devices.

The rain persisted, and in fact became more and more vio-lent. On the next day, the rest of the Plumbesses left the Orphanage to help nearby villages. Roc was leaving too, but she told her apprentice first.

"Zag left about a week ago to help a village with this storm. Flotsam, I think the place was called. We've known that it was a serious storm for a while now, but to think it would make it all the way to the Orphanage . . . I'll be back soon, girl."

"Is there anything I can do to help?" Seg asked.

"Just keep your eye on things around here. Especially the servants—gods know they need strict oversight. That will be enough."

That afternoon, Seg was watching Eck roll around in the mud when a very urgent noise came out of one of the pipe-grams. Not a single Plumbess was around, so she went to answer it herself.

The message was brief. It said, "Zag here. Terrible flooding. I can save Flotsam if you save me. Hurry."

Seg was frantically trying to figure out how the valves of the Sump worked when Eck appeared beside her.

"What are you doing?" Eck asked.

"Zag's in trouble," she said. "I've got to help her." She finally decided on a valve and took it in hand.

"They told us not to touch any of the valves," Eck said.

"Well, yeah, that's because it's 'terribly dangerous' or something like that. It's called the Sump, and apparently only a Plumbess can use it without poisoning the Orphanage." She then began to turn.

Eck's hand was immediately on her wrist, stopping her from opening the valve any farther.

"Let go," Seg demanded.

"You just said yourself that only a Plumbess can use it safely. You're not a Plumbess."

"Zag's in trouble!" Seg yelled. "And there isn't a single Plumbess here! Only I can do this."

"You're not a Plumbess," Eck repeated quietly, firmly.

Seg tried to pull her wrist free, but Eck held on. She looked weak—she'd somehow gone without food and water for three weeks—but Seg's diet hadn't been much better, and Eck's grip was strangely firm. So Seg tried to hit her, which resulted in them tumbling to the ground, where they continued struggling against each other.

Seg felt very near to winning—she had her hand around Eck's throat—when an increasingly loud rumble interrupted them.

The entire room was shaking. Seg looked at the lead pipe to Flotsam and watched helplessly as it ripped itself free from its housing and—disappeared.

"Agh!" Seg yelled, and struggled to her feet. She stumbled to the wall where the pipe had been and opened all the valves. Nothing happened. There was, however, another message on the readout. It said, "Goodbye."

"Look what you've done!" she yelled at Eck.

Eck slowly got to her own feet, her hand feeling at her injured neck. "You almost killed me," she said.

Seg was so angry that she took her plunger and used it like she never had before—to strike a person.

Eck fell to the ground, a weak, malnourished girl.

"I could've saved her!" Seg yelled.

Eck slowly got to her feet again, the side of her face turning into a bruise. "No, you couldn't have," she said, with a confidence only she could have. "This place," she said, "it's a drain. I can tell that much. You don't know drains like I do—and even I don't understand it."

Seg pointed her plunger at Eck.

"What are you going to do?" Eck asked.

"If you don't leave, I swear I'll kill you."

"If you say so," Eck said, and left.

When Roc returned a day later, it was to a wasted scene. Eck was gone and Seg had confined herself to her room, where she would be for ten days—watching the rain as it fell.

PIPES TO DREAMS

ECK SCRIBBLED THE blueprint of her drain, the work of her life, onto the first thing that came to hand, which happened to be a dinner napkin. It only contained broad strokes, initial placement and general design considerations, but she discussed a lot of the minutia with the engineer men at her disposal and they nodded their heads a lot.

The engineer men, always zealous, were quick to break ground. They had enormous machines for digging, and used high-pressure water to disintegrate any rock that got in the way. They brought in enormous pipes that had to be lowered by winches; they folded huge sheets of copper, and even lead. It was an enormous undertaking.

So enormous that, after telling them what to do, there wasn't much else for Eck to contribute. She couldn't lift the pipes, and the machines far outpaced her shoveling abilities.

So, to distract herself and avoid too much introspection, she instead turned to another project, one she could oversee and perform personally. In fact, she told no one about it, even Pipe Lord Marcus. He didn't seem to like a lot of her ideas, and she wasn't in an emotional state to handle rejection.

Her project also happened to be modifying his throne, which he probably wouldn't appreciate either. She worked in the middle of the night, or, if she was feeling brave, in the time between court sessions. A lot of the barons and baronesses took naps. She also kept it inconspicuous, a small weld here or there and slow, silent Plumbing. Just like she'd done in the graveyard.

No one had discovered her modifications to the graveyard yet, but that was likely because no one went there anymore. She had changed it, made it desolate, forlorn, and although the people of the town didn't realize why they avoided it, they avoided it nonetheless. Eck had ruined their place of mourning. If there were actually any bodies in it, she would've felt worse, but still she had shame.

So she was more careful, and put a little more hope into her work. Marcus wouldn't just start avoiding his throne like people had started avoiding the graveyard—he would find out what was wrong with it, and the Plumbing would be easily traced back to her. If it turned out well, she'd tell him then.

That was what she focused on—making it well. And she followed Quemar's advice: she got lost in the work. Even though it wasn't a drain, not really, she found happiness inside. She almost felt pride, sometimes—a slow, burning fire. She stoked that and spent all the time she could working on it.

Of course, the weather at the Manor of Storms refused to give her time. It sabotaged the city daily, and made Marcus impatient with her. "After seeing what you did with the library, I thought you'd have things under better control," he told her.

"That was only a temporary solution," she reminded him. "I had to convince it to behave. At any moment it could revert and the damage would be redone. The only permanent solution is the drain we're working on."

Even though the graveyard was helping, she didn't tell him about it for the same reason she didn't tell him about the throne. Best to let the drains do their silent work, best to let the rumors float.

On a day when Marcus was particularly harsh with her, she skipped second court and spent the evening walking about the city, looking for draining solutions. Nothing suggested itself. She'd almost given up and returned to her garden when she was fallen upon by a stranger. She never even saw the woman coming.

"Please," the woman said, and grabbed at Eck's black sleeve with a desperate hand. "Please, you have to help me."

They were in some dark alley. Like almost everywhere else in the Manor, it was too stagnant to drain properly. Eck didn't have to look down to know there was blood flowing down the woman's legs, pooling on the ground. She could smell it. The woman's other hand clasped at a swollen belly.

"Please, help," she repeated.

"It can birth itself," Eck whispered, muted by fear.

"Please," the woman cried, pulling her closer, into the blood and the smell and the fear. "There's something wrong, Plumbess. Please help with the baby."

"I don't know how!" Eck screamed. "I don't know how, I don't know how, I DON'T KNOW HOW!"

It took force to break the woman's grasp, and it took considerable effort to run away from such desperation. But she did. And after that, she didn't wear her Plumbess outfit in public.

She wore her blue dress instead, the one that made her feel like a snake. It seemed like the perfect plan—everybody avoided snakes. Nobody expected anything good from snakes. A Plumbess, on the other hand, was nothing but expectations. People wanted a Plumbess to drain endless rivers and then blamed her for the drowning; people wanted a Plumbess to deliver endless children and then blamed her for the clogs. She would be a snake again.

The plan had a fatal flaw, though—she'd forgotten about Baron Marlow. About a week before, he'd slipped into a perfect silence, so the nobility let him out of his room every now and then. For the most part, he was as harmless as he sounded. He just wandered the halls, waved out windows, and ate the occasional food. Eck had seen him a few times, and he'd ignored her like she didn't exist.

But when she crossed his path again in a dark Manor hallway, when he saw her in her blue dress, the same one she'd worn to the ball, recognition lit in his eyes. His jaw slackened like a snake preparing to swallow much larger prey.

"Woman," he croaked, and extended an arm out toward her.

Eck froze, for reasons she didn't understand. Then he took one of those jarring, irrevocable steps toward her, and she found herself again. A searing anger, unlike anything she'd ever felt before, melted her back into action. This time, she had her plunger. She lashed out, and found herself so deep in his mind that, for a moment, she was disoriented.

Rotting things surrounded her, walls covered in filth and a slow pulse that pumped poison in an endless circuit, keeping time. She could feel it all—the rotten dreams, the sodden thoughts like yellowed teeth. She hated all of it.

Without a thought as to what she did, she raised her plunger like a lightning rod and called the dark waters upon her. She called the filth, the waste, the runoff, all the sordid things people tried to force down drains and forget about. She demanded them to her, and they listened. Like a toxic wave they crashed down, threatening to drown her, but she didn't break—still she held her plunger up and called deeper.

She penetrated into the despair of humanity, primal fears, into the essential loneliness of existence, the abysmal depths of loss—she saw Seg there and nearly lost her tidal pull—into a fear of death that she never knew was so pervasive, so fundamental. And everywhere she penetrated she left a conduit directly into the man who had touched her.

When she opened her eyes again, she shouldn't have been surprised to see such a thoroughly destroyed human—but she was. Marlow's eyes had rolled back into his head, and his skin had become a fetid brown. He was foaming at the mouth and his body was wracked by powerful spasms.

"Excuse me," she said, and stepped around him.

She was ashamed to realize that she felt better, after that. Lighter. Light enough to check the progress of her drain. So she strolled out to where it made its bold mark on the earth.

The drain was placed as close to the Fountain as Marcus

would allow—he'd said something about it offending the aesthetic, and she'd tried explaining to him that a drain's effectiveness was proportional to its proximity, and the Fountain seemed to be the source of a lot of trouble. She walked toward their compromise.

The sky was overcast, but a small ray of light broke through the clouds. Had that been there before?

She found Eric hard at work. "How's the progress?" she asked.

"Plumbess," he said, "I haven't seen you in days. I was beginning to worry about you."

"I'm all right," she said, and felt it to be true. "But tell me how the drain is."

"We're deeper now than we've ever been before, but we're overcoming all the obstacles," he said. "We are finding snakes down there, though. Were you aware of that?"

She nodded. "Yes, they'll be everywhere by now. Don't worry about them. I'll keep them under control."

"If you say so."

They both looked down for a while, thoughts lost in the drain. Then he said, "Listen, Eck." He sounded hesitant. "There's something I've wanted to talk to you about."

"Oh," she said. "What's that?"

He looked around at his fellow engineer men and then said, "I have some ideas about the drain. Walk with me?"

The last thing Eck wanted to hear was a change to her plan, but she followed him anyway.

When they were out of earshot of the other engineer men, Eric said, "The Orphanage has been trying to contact you through the pipegram. Someone named Roc."

"Roc? I thought you said you wanted to talk about the drain?"

"One of the engineers," he continued, "was instructed to destroy the messages. I don't know who, but I have my suspicions."

"What? Why would they do that?"

"I hate to say it, but some of the engineers are . . . are jealous of you. And they wouldn't hesitate to collude against a Plumbess."

"I'll tell Marcus," she said. "He'll take care of it."

"No!" Eric yelled, rather loudly. Then, quieter, he said, "No. I didn't tell you this so that you would go telling anyone else, including the Pipe Lord. For all I know, he's the one who ordered them to destroy the messages. Only him and a few barons have the authority to use the pipegram. I told you so you would be aware, so you could look out."

"But if I can't trust Marcus, I can't trust anyone," she said.

"That seems a little exaggerated."

"Three years ago, he came to the Orphanage to find *me*. He said he needed *me*. And if someone needs me, then . . . then I need them. I don't have anyone else."

"You can trust me," Eric said.

Eck's face became uncharacteristically blank, her hand clenched around her plunger. She asked, in a strangely cold tone, "Are you jealous of me?"

"Wha—what?"

"You said some of the engineer men were jealous of me, and you're an engineer man. Are you jealous of me?"

He got angry. "Fine! If your precious Pipe Lord is all you need, go to him. I was only trying to help, but I'm just an *engi-*

neer man, a Plumber man, nothing at all. Go to the Pipe Lord."

And he walked away.

Later that night, after second court, she did just that. Or tried to, at least. After a speech by Baron Porb about the smell of lavender, she started to ask about the messages, but was immediately interrupted by a baroness.

"I've had it!" the baroness yelled. "Simply had it! Two months I put up with whatever happened to Baron Marlow. I bore it out of the kindness of my heart. But now your Plumbess has broken him even more. I don't know how and I don't know why, but she did. He just twitches and foams—he's hardly alive at all. You need to resolve this, my lord. You need to fix your baron."

The clamor of nobility departing stopped—everyone wanted to hear what was said.

Marcus looked down at the baroness with passionless eyes. "If you're concerned about the baron's health, you should consult a doctor. They are, after all, the health professionals."

"Do you think I haven't done that!?" the baroness replied. "Three doctors, each more confounded than the last. The last one told me I should try sunning him more. Sunning!"

Another person, apparently deciding the time was at hand, joined in. "Snakes! Snakes everywhere! It's not natural!"

"There's something horribly wrong with this Plumbess!" yelled another.

"Snakes aren't natural?" Eck hissed, but Marcus was the only person close enough to hear.

"Silence!" he yelled, and silence came. The thrumming of the Fountain reigned. "I will not," he said, "tolerate complaints against my Plumbess. She's doing everything she can to improve our Manor. Baron Marlow, if he is an upstanding gentleman, will conquer his illness. Now, is there anything else any of you wish to say?"

No one responded.

"You're dismissed, all of you," he said.

Eck went to bed alone that night—she'd sent every snake she knew into the sewers, to keep things under control. She also went to bed furious. For hours she tossed and turned under her rose bush, scratching herself on its thorns.

Even when she finally fell asleep, she slid straight into a restless nightmare.

An infinitely long pipe extended into the sky, and on its other end was Marlow, transfixed. She stood right next to him, and his eyes bulged in terror of her. The refuse of humanity still flowed directly into him and his body metabolized it, although poorly.

Around them stood the jealous engineer men, the gossiping courtiers, the stablemen who saw fit to kill horses. Her hatred bloomed hard, a flower of death, and, caught in its grasp, she piped all of them—she reached for more infinitely long pipes, for hundreds of them, and thrust them through the mind of everyone she could reach.

They tried to run away from her, but they were no match. The dream was a pipe, and she was a Plumbess. The result was a field of piped people, a septic tank where they were the bacteria. She smiled at her creation.

To the baroness who accused her of breaking Marlow, she said, "This is your chance to help him. Share his burden. If you do a good enough job, he might survive."

She woke to clear skies—for the first time ever, sunlight

reached her garden through crystal windows. Although she wasn't well rested, she felt lighter. She got dressed, and tried to go see how the rest of the Manor looked.

The door to her garden was once again valveless—she pulled on the handle, but nothing happened. It bothered her less this time.

"Another thing to ask Marcus about," she said. As long as she had a drain, she would be fine.

Soon she was out in the hallways, the ones that never seemed to go anywhere. And she saw the result of her work. A lot of the people just looked a little nauseous, pausing to lean on the occasional wall, but some of them looked as bad as Marlow. None of them acknowledged her, as if she didn't exist to them. She could live with that.

She made it to the throne room just in time for first court—bells marked the time as she walked through the archway—but no one was there except Marcus.

The weather seemed to have lightened his mood as well. "I haven't seen the Manor this bright in years," he said, smiling.

"I might've had something to do with that," she said.

"Then you really are everything I hoped for. You're wonderful, Eck. I'm sorry for the mood I've been in lately, the things I've said. It's just the weather."

Eck blushed furiously. Then, since he seemed so happy and first court looked like it wouldn't happen, she took the opportunity to ask. "Marcus, I have a question."

"Go ahead," he said. He seemed distracted, though. He was twisted in his throne, looking back at the Fountain.

"Did you tell an engineer man to destroy messages sent to me by the Orphanage?"

A moment of complete silence, but then he started focusing on her better. "What makes you ask that, Eck?"

"Oh, Eric told me you might have done that. But he said a lot of other things, too. Did you?"

"I would never, Eck."

She reflected on the problem better now—she'd released a lot of frustration she didn't know she had, and it had cleared her mind. She looked down at her plunger. "I think I can probably solve this on my own, actually. In fact, I know I can. Sorry for bothering you."

"You know," he said, "I can have someone look into it myself. You don't have to trouble yourself with things like that. You've got your drain to worry about."

"It's fine, Marcus. I can handle it."

"If you say so," he said. "But do let me know what you find out."

She made her cheery way to the valve house, where she found two men manning the valves. Both foamed at the mouth.

"Very sorry," she said, by way of conversation. Neither of them responded. She went to the pipegram, but instead of using the valves, she approached the lead pipe itself. It stretched nearly as long as the pipe in her dreams—she could feel its tremendous weight. She touched it with her bare hand, and then, gaining confidence, struck it with her plunger.

The vibration was strong. On its other end she could feel the Orphanage, someone listening, someone about to respond.

"Plumbess?" a voice said, startling her.

"Oh!" she exclaimed. "You scared me." It was an engineer man, she could tell by his silly hat. "Is there something you need?" she asked.

"There's a problem with the drain," he told her. "We think you should come and take a look at it."

She looked one last time at the lead pipe, but then turned to the engineer man. Whatever had happened to the messages, it seemed relatively unimportant. The drain would be her life-work, the thing that would make Marcus happy. What could matter more?

"Okay," she said. "Let's hurry."

The sky outside was dimming—she had the fleeting thought that she should attach more people to her septic system, but then her thoughts turned entirely to the drain. As she got near, she could tell something was very wrong. She didn't know what or why, but she very much knew it. Something dark, something ominous.

"Did someone die?" she asked the engineer man.

"Best to see it for yourself," he said.

At the mouth of the drain, Marcus stood staring down into its abyss. She approached him first.

"What happened?" she asked.

"Nothing I can't fix," he said. "Can I see your plunger?"

"Of course." It was unusual, the request, but her trust ran deep.

He looked at it for a moment, almost longingly, and then he dropped it into the drain.

Eck watched it fall in disbelief. Marcus took her by the arm, bare in her snake dress.

She reacted like she had with Baron Marlow—confused, but always ready to defend herself. She struck at his mind and tried to repipe it, but she found herself in a deluge, lightning crashing down, with Marcus's twisted face smiling down on her, derisive.

She was gasping for breath. She was drowning.

"I'm sorry, Eck," his voice thundered down on her. "I was hoping you'd get farther with the drain. But fate has moved the timetables."

Desperate, she reached for her necklace, the one given to her by Quemar, and broke its chain. "Here," she said, "eat this."

Marcus just laughed. "That's absurd, Eck. I'm not going to do that. But I will take it—I know to value a keepsake."

His hand was now firmly around her neck, holding her over the drain. She managed to gasp one last question.

"Why?"

"For the Dry Princess," he said, and let go.

* * * * * * *

After hours of furious activity, Marcus settled back on his throne, exhausted. Immediately after Eck had voiced her suspicions about the messages, he'd held a quick meeting with what was left of his engineers—to make sure they could build it on their own. Then he'd disposed of both Eck and the head engineer. His plans were too fragile to withstand much outside force—it was what he had to do.

And then he'd set up a dormitory for the people Eck had attached to pipes. His engineers said that as long as they were alive, they would help with the Manor's draining problem. He would keep them alive, at least long enough to finish the drain.

He was deep in thought about the future when a servant walked into the throne room, escorting a little boy.

"I'm busy," Marcus said.

"But my lord," the boy replied, "I've found a leak."

Marcus was so preoccupied with his draining problem that he took the statement literally. "Where?" he asked. "Where is it this time?"

The boy was confused. "Where? She . . . she said it didn't matter where, just that there was a leak. And that I recommend Plumbess Seg."

THE WORK OF A PLUMBESS

WITH THE OBSTRUCTION gone, the drain took on a different shape. Seg was caught up in its current, completely at its mercy—she prayed that it deposited her somewhere tolerable.

After decades, after days of draining, Seg surfaced in a grey-water pond surrounded by trees. She must've been far from Hope Springs—she hadn't seen trees, or a standing body of water, in months.

She waded to the pool's edge, where she straightened her outfit back out. Then she got her bearings. She could feel, in the distance, the weak pulse of a town. The Plumbing was calling to her, she supposed—a song she was beginning to hear. She walked in that direction.

The town, she noticed, had all the opposite problems of Hope Springs. Its streets and buildings were washed out, its people muddied. She walked through and past all of it, toward her ultimate destination: another statue of a Plumbess, standing alone at the town's far edge.

How many statues would there be? How many Plumbesses immortalized in stone yet doomed to obscurity? At least this one wasn't dead, like the statues back in the Obstruction's crypt. Water still flowed through her fountain, and her features were freshly carved. The plaque at her feet still bore her name: Plumbess Zag. There she was again. Always so close, always permanently lost.

Seg was standing there, mostly lost herself, when a man interrupted her tragedy.

"So you're a Plumbess too?"

Seg looked down at herself, perhaps wondering the same thing. For some reason, her broken Lead was still in her left hand. She turned it over with her fingers, catching a dull glint of light.

Yes, she was a Plumbess.

"Did you know her?" he asked, gesturing at the statue.

She just nodded. Then she asked a question she already knew the answer to. "Where am I?"

"Flotsam," the man said. "Or at least what's left of it."

Flotsam. The town Zag had died trying to save. Seg had drained a long way.

"Did you ever find her body?" she asked, and filled the question with the last irrational hope she had—that Zag was still out there somewhere, alive and well.

The man recognized and dismissed her hope. "No, we lost her body like we lost so many other things. But I saw myself how she was struck by lightning at least a dozen times. I've never seen anything like it. She's gone."

With a growing conviction that she knew exactly where she was—not just in Flotsam, not just on the other side of a difficult drain, but, rather, on her way toward the real Obstruction—she asked, "And the Manor of Storms is nearby? Pipe Lord Marcus?"

The man darkened. "You've come to work for him, I suppose."

"I would never." Seg felt an anger growing, with an inertia that would never stop.

"Oh . . . good. I mean, excuse me for saying it, but a lot of people around here think he caused the flooding. And, as terrifying as it is to admit, I think the worst is yet to come."

"Can I . . . can I please have just one moment alone with her?"

"Of course, Plumbess."

She heard his footsteps retreat, but she never looked away from the hollow gaze of the Plumbess. When she knew she was alone, she said, "So this is what you gave your life for, Zag? A little town like this? Was it worth the risk?"

The statue didn't answer.

"I'm in some deep waters myself. Again. Eck saved me last time, but I get the feeling that this time it's my turn. I've risked so much, and I haven't saved anyone."

She took her broken Lead and placed it in Zag's outstretched hand. "But I suppose I can risk a little more."

She turned around and found that hundreds of people surrounded her, sharing her silence. She might've been surprised, but she wasn't.

To the man who'd spoken to her before, she said, "I'll make you a deal, Flotsam. I'll take care of your Pipe Lord. I'll make sure he never causes such terrible waste again. All I ask in return . . ."

She thought about Plumbess Mar, lonely and dry, with only a solitary baron and a senile Pipe Lord holding on to her memory. Mar's statue must've looked like this forty years ago. Could Zag, who meant everything to her, really suffer the same fate? She thought as well about the empty crypt, the nameless centuries of Plumbesses with their plaques erased. Was it all really a cycle?

"All I ask is that you keep the water in this fountain flowing, for as long as this town lives," Seg continued. "And that you'll . . . that you'll remember her."

She knew the man could see the sadness in her, so heavy. And yet he said, "You don't have to ask for that, Plumbess. Believe me when I say that she means as much to us as she does to you. She saved us."

When Roc had said those same words the day Seg left the Orphanage, Seg hadn't believed her. She'd felt so very alone in her pain, in her grief. But now they seemed like the only words that mattered.

She smiled. "Well, promise me anyway."

"Okay, Plumbess."

"There's one more thing I must ask for, I suppose. Can someone get me an orphan?"

Someone did. A little boy was produced, and Seg proceeded as she was bound to: she knelt down to his level, asked for his name, and told him everything he needed to know to bring the Pipe Lord to her. She took a spare glove out of her bag and pressed it into his hands. "And make sure he takes this. Good luck."

After the boy had disappeared on the stormed horizon, Seg went about finding a task to do while she waited. Flotsam's problems seemed to be entirely of the draining sort, so she wasn't surprised to learn that they were having difficulties with their toilets.

"Show me the worst one," Seg said.

"But Plumbess, you really shouldn't trouble yourself with—"

"Nonsense," Seg said. "It's what I do. As bad as it is, I assure you, I've dealt with worse."

She was very nearly proven wrong—the toilet shown to her was about as bad as they could get. And yet, Seg was happy. Happy to be Plumbing again. And so she plunged in, putting her anger to good use. She'd just finished when a black carriage appeared on the horizon, bringing rain in its wake.

She walked out to meet it, so that the townsfolk of Flotsam didn't have to suffer the moisture. The carriage pulled to a stop before her, and liverymen much darker and more graceful than Carral's opened the door. Pipe Lord Marcus descended.

"Plumbess Seg," he said. "It's been so long. I hope time has treated you well."

He extended his right hand, and she met it with hers. He didn't fail to notice that her hand was gloved. He took the one given to him by the orphan and tossed it aside. "So this isn't a Service Call, then. I feel I've been deceived."

"One good Plumbess is more than even a Pipe Lord can hope for in a lifetime," Seg said. "And I know you have Eck."

His eyes glimmered—she could feel waves behind them. "There's no hiding anything from a Plumbess, is there? I've thought for a while now that the Orphanage might send someone here looking for her. Yes, she came to me—seeking refuge. It was her wish to remain hidden."

Seg knew the lie, but didn't acknowledge it. "I only came to talk to her. We were friends, in the Orphanage."

"Just to talk with an old friend? Then I hope you'll accept a ride back to my Manor, where I'm sure that could be arranged."

"Gladly," she said.

She declined the help of the liveryman, and climbed of her own accord up into the carriage. Marcus climbed in behind her, and soon the carriage swung into motion.

She looked out the window at the drowning countryside. "Seems wet around here," she said.

"Not to complain," Marcus replied, "but I brought my draining problem to the attention of the Orphanage years ago."

"And the Orphanage paid for your problem with a life," Seg said.

He tensed.

"Didn't you know that?" she pressed. "Plumbess Zag. She died in the town we just left, only a few months ago."

"I'm . . . I'm sorry for your loss," he eventually said.

"*Our* loss," she corrected.

The carriage emerged from the valley, and Seg found herself immersed in a nightmare. Rain fell in curtains to the ground, and pipes tore unnaturally at the sky. It was an abomination; something that should never have existed.

"What have you done?" she said, breathless.

"Aren't you impressed?" he asked. "The lifework of Plumbess Sol, and now Eck has contributed equally. The greatest marvel of Plumbing the world has ever seen."

"Eck would never contribute to something like this," Seg replied.

"Are you so sure about that?"

Against her will, she thought about it. How well did she know Eck? She remembered how easily the girl had fallen prey to Marcus's praise years ago. Would Eck really help build something like this, just to impress him? Perhaps she didn't recognize the danger.

"I know what she could be," Seg finally said. "I know she's above all of this, and above you. I know that if I talked to her, I could convince her of that."

"If you're so confident you'll deprive me of my Plumbess," he said, "it's strange that you think I would just let you do it."

"You offered me a ride," Seg said.

"I'm confident myself," he replied. Then, as if confidence wasn't enough, he said, "You're scared of it, aren't you. Of what Plumbing can really do. I've always thought it funny that the Orphanage is so *weak*, just a couple of old women and motherless children. Do we really bow to that, we who are capable of so much? Look at my Fountain. Really look at it. What does the Orphanage have to rival its splendor? You hoard all the world's knowledge, yes, and act like it makes you holy, but look what I made anyway. Look what I made *despite* you. I'm not so easily restrained, no—I am the Pipe Lord of the Manor of Storms."

"Good for you," Seg said.

After that they were silent, the only sound made by the gathering rain. Marcus stared at her plunger a lot, and for her part she stared at the floor. Eventually the carriage stopped, and the door was opened.

Marcus got out first, and she followed. She alighted at the foot of the enormous Fountain. It was a monstrosity, a perversion of everything Plumbing was supposed to be.

The Pipe Lord was walking away, off toward a huge, terrible building on the other side of the Fountain. "Enjoy your stay," he called back to her.

"Where's Eck?" she yelled after him.

"Probably working on her drain," he replied, and then he disappeared up a staircase.

It wasn't a very helpful answer, but Seg didn't mind being rid of him. She could find things on her own. She went to the nearest pipe and struck it with her plunger. It made the sound of a gavel, an indictment against the blasphemy around her. She adjusted and struck again, and this time heard a drain in the distance. She followed its slow, melancholy sound and found an enormous hole in the ground not too far from the Fountain.

Dozens of men were at work there, carrying around materials and operating heavy machinery.

"Eck, where are you?" she yelled. "Have any of you seen Eck?"

None of them acknowledged her. The rain redoubled. Frustrated, she struck a random, sinister piece of machinery with her plunger and, to her surprise, it shattered. An enormous snake slid out of it, landing at her feet.

"Damned snakes," a nearby man said and, with the blade of a shovel he carried, struck its head off. A rivulet caught the severed head and carried it over the edge of the drain.

Without even considering the consequences, Seg jumped in after it. She fell just as fast as a snake's head—that was gravity. The head was just out of her reach, plunging deeper and deeper into the massive drain, a drain larger than any Seg had ever even dreamed about. It dwarfed Mar's drain. It swallowed Seg whole.

Soon, she became afraid of the speed at which she was falling. She used her plunger to slow herself and, at the fathomless bottom, came to a stop.

The rain penetrated even to such depths—large drops of it pounded her forehead as she looked up. She took her candle from her bag and lit it, shielding its fragile flame with her hand. Then she looked around at the morbid scene that presented itself.

Severed limbs were everywhere, human pieces of various shapes and sizes. What was wrong with this place?

"Eck, where are you?" she called.

She heard a dying cough and rushed to a broken body huddled in a bleak corner of the pipe. Hope flared up in her only to be extinguished. It was a man.

"Are you . . . are you a Plumbess?" he asked when she turned him over. He wasn't going to live.

"I came to save Eck," she told him.

"I tried to warn her," he said, coughing blood. "Tell her I'm sorry."

There seemed to be a story behind those words, but Seg didn't care what it was. She forged onward, into the pipe's insane depths. She called Eck's name, she stepped over massacred bodies. Deeper than she hoped to go, she heard a crying and rushed forward once more.

It was the high-pitched crying of a newborn. She found it half-buried in a pile of severed arms, right next to the crumpled, cold body of Eck.

"Oh, Eck," she cried, dropping to her knees next to her lost friend. "I tried to be there for you. I came. I'm here. I'm sorry, Eck, I should've, I should've—"

The tragedy of her life was interrupted by a searing pain in her neck. A snake, larger than any she'd ever seen, held her in its jaws and coiled itself around her torso. It began to constrict, threatening to break all of her bones at once.

She didn't struggle. Instead, she did what she should've done years before—she embraced it. She whispered to the head embedded in her neck, "If you trust in me, I can make this right. Let me make this right."

The crushing stopped, the snake uncoiled. Slowly, painfully, it withdrew its fangs from her neck.

"Thank you," she said.

She picked up the baby and told it, "Come on, let's get out of here. This is no place for you."

She looked up the shaft of the drain and knew it was impossible—a drain of such magnitude only went down. But she wasn't defeated. She took her plunger and stuck it to the wall. Then she put her ear up to its handle and listened over the cries of the inconsolable baby.

She heard the unmistakable sound of the lead pipe that led to the Orphanage. It wouldn't help her, but it was still a curiosity—apparently Eck couldn't resist tying such a powerful drain into her Plumbing. Seg unstuck her plunger and repeated the process on the opposite wall.

There, she heard what she was hoping for. She took her ear away from the plunger's handle and struck it with her palm, driving it through the wall of the pipe. It pierced through to a nearby artery—the one supplying the Fountain.

Water sprayed out violently. With the baby tightly in her arms, she strode against it, her plunger shielding them both. Then she dove in. The artery took her to the heart, to the

Fountain at the surface. Frantically she swam to the edge of its voluminous waters, keeping the baby's head safely up. She found an edge to hold on to, and then turned her full attention to the baby.

"You made it," she said. "You made it."

Numbness was radiating from the wounds in her neck, and her thoughts were becoming clouded. But she couldn't give up yet. Exhausted, she heaved herself up and out of the Fountain and descended into a crowd of people.

They were dressed like nobility, like barons and baronesses, but they couldn't have been uglier. They were mere caricatures of people shoved into fancy suits and low-cut dresses. The garish makeup they wore did nothing to conceal their fundamental indecency.

Many of them were coughing, a phlegmy cough that bespoke true sickness. Around these people she could sense the aura of a pipe, filling them with waste. She could also sense that it was a Plumbess's work. Had Eck done that?

Marcus, the Pipe Lord, stood among them. His look of nobility was more convincing, but Seg could see the death behind it.

To the gathered crowd, he proclaimed, "What did I tell you? She's come here to wreak havoc. She's sabotaged the Fountain."

The anger in his voice wasn't feigned—the Fountain was, in fact, suffering from arterial bleeding, and Seg had made the incision.

"Tell me, intruder, what have you done with our Plumbess? What have you done with Eck?" he demanded.

"What have *I* done with Eck?" she replied, but her voice

was muted by dizziness. The holes in her neck drained nothingness into the vessel of her body.

"The first thing you did when you came here was ask where she was—what have you done?"

Seg couldn't respond.

"I thought as much," he continued. "I was foolish to trust you, foolish to bring you to our Manor. She has killed our Plumbess!"

The crowd displayed a strange mixture of indignation and relief.

"Engineers, seize her," Marcus said, and two men grabbed her by the arms. "Take her to the throne room, where she will receive judgment."

She struggled to keep hold of the baby as she was tossed about—it took almost all the strength she had. She knew, under a gauze of nothing, that she was about to die, but she could only manage enough concern for the baby. Someone had to take care of it. And although no one decent was around, she had to work with the materials at hand.

To a frog of a baron walking alongside her as she was dragged, she said, "Please, sir, take this child. Make sure she finds a good home."

He ignored her.

"Please," she said to a bloated baroness, "is there no compassion in you? Someone has to take care of this child."

She, too, ignored Seg.

With the last of her words, she declaimed, "If you, who have so much, are incapable of this small act of humanity, if you won't extend a hand to a helpless child in need, then you're already forever damned. Can this really be the case?"

No one replied. If Seg had been her full self, and if there wasn't the heavy weight of a child in her arms, a weight that needed special tending, she would've destroyed all of them with her plunger. Instead, she was dragged up a staircase, through audacious hallways, and into an equally decadent throne room.

Marcus was already seated in his throne, backed by the view of the diminished Fountain. Seg almost couldn't believe what she was seeing, but as she was dragged closer, as she was cast at his feet, she was absolutely certain: the throne Marcus sat on was a drain. He couldn't have known, or else he wouldn't have looked so comfortable. It was a rather powerful drain.

"Give me her plunger," Marcus said, and an engineer tried pulling it unkindly from her hand. She let it go.

The Plumbing of the throne drain was subtle, probably only discernable to a Plumbess. And Seg felt with certainty that she recognized the work: Eck had made it. But it was a different side of Eck—it wasn't the same Eck who'd designed the enormous drain that Seg had fallen into. It was a happier Eck, an optimistic Eck. It, too, was Plumbed to the lead pipe of the Orphanage—Eck really couldn't resist the pull of that heavy drain.

A real work. It somehow made Seg happy to see it, and even brought a weak smile to her face. Her lips moved, but made no sound. She would've said, "You're wonderful, Eck. You're beautiful, Eck."

Marcus declared, his voice resounding in the room's great void, "It pains me to see such treachery from what was once a venerable institution. The Orphanage isn't what it used to be. Rats, all of you. Do you have anything to say in your defense before you are judged?"

Eck gave Seg the strength she needed to end it. "The Dry Princess will never choose you," she said.

"Excuse me?" That struck a nerve.

"You're weak, and from my understanding, she doesn't like weakness."

"Does this look like weakness to you?" he asked, encompassing the whole Manor of Storms with a defiant gesture. Behind him the Fountain continued to struggle.

"If you were truly strong," she replied, "you wouldn't be so afraid of a Plumbess with a plunger."

"Here," he said. "I will gladly prove you wrong before you die, Plumbess." He took her plunger from the engineer and lowered it down to where she knelt shakily on the floor. "Are you even alive enough to hold it?" he asked.

She reached out and grabbed it by the handle. She was immediately surrounded by a raging storm, by pipes that fell to the ground like hail. And Marcus stood in the middle of it, undaunted, a sneer playing widely across his face. It was like the nightmare from years before, the one that had nearly killed her. A familiar place. But this time she yelled, "Do you even understand Plumbing, Pipe Lord?"

His sneer cracked.

"Do you not even recognize the drain you're sitting on?" she said, and watched as his confidence faltered. Then she summoned all her remaining power and opened the valve to his throne.

The drain was so powerful that it pulled all of the rain into its tremendous orbit. It was so powerful that it siphoned all the poison from Seg's neck, which had been so close to killing her. But it wasn't powerful enough to drain Marcus. It had him in its jaws, at the very edge of its abyss, but it couldn't swallow him.

Seg, for her part, could only barely hold on to the plunger that kept her anchored to safety—she only had one hand. The other held the baby, still clenched tightly at her chest. Only a few meters separated her from where Marcus struggled to keep from draining.

Even struggling, Marcus laughed. "You Plumbesses are almost more trouble than you're worth," he said. "Did Eck do this?"

Seg had no more words for him. She had enough to deal with—water was pouring in around her, threatening to drown her again. She didn't have much time.

She pulled her plunger free from its mooring, and then made a single, pleading strike against the ground. She directed it at the lead pipe somewhere deep in the drain's Plumbing. Then she anchored her plunger again. Even just one second exposed to the drain's pull had brought her half the distance to Marcus.

Moments later, a message came—just vibrations in a pipe, but Seg could understand them. They said, "The Orphanage listens."

To respond, to make the necessary vibrations, Seg had to let go again, and for longer. But it was a risk she was ready to take. She pulled herself free again and, as the drain pulled her, struck out the words, "Save me, Roc."

She fell into Marcus. He smiled at her, baring all his teeth.

Seg surrendered herself completely to her leaden fate and the understanding it carried. It was heavy, ungodly, but it rewarded her with a vision of what Eck should have done, what she could still do. She tore the necklace from around Marcus's neck and shoved it into his open mouth.

"Eat this."

Then the Sump turned on, and she saw the confidence die in his eyes. His fingers started to slip and his mouth to foam. Seg pushed herself up and away from him with her legs, giving her just enough distance to perform a single, solid strike of the plunger to his face. It sent him draining once and for all.

Her plunger was the only thing that kept her from falling after him. The Sump stopped, and she emerged from the struggle to find herself alone in the throne room. Outside, the sun shone down on an empty fountain.

Seg collapsed and only just avoided falling on the child crying in her arms.

She awoke in Hope Springs, to the sound of people cheering her name—the drain was clear; the child was found.

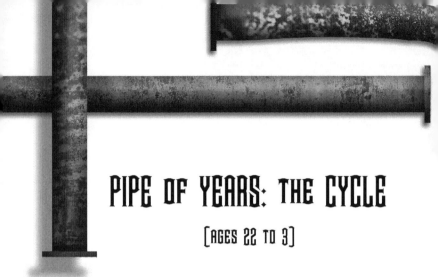

PIPE OF YEARS: THE CYCLE
[AGES 22 TO 3]

THREE YEARS WENT by before Seg returned to the Orphanage. Someone must have seen her coming, because Roc met her at the gate.

Seg embraced her old mentor, and Roc, although awkwardly, returned the embrace.

"You've certainly kept me waiting long enough," Roc said. "When you said you were coming, I thought you meant it."

"I had work to finish," Seg said. "And we took the long way." She looked down at the little girl by her side.

"What's her name, then?" Roc asked.

"Well, I thought about naming her after Zag," Seg said, "but her temperament is completely different. She's so very domineering."

Roc cackled. "They're always a handful at that age, and for years to come."

"She certainly finds all my nerves," Seg agreed. "I can almost forgive you for being annoyed with raising me."

"Almost is good enough for me. I suppose you think you love her, then?"

"Yeah, I love her." Seg winced as the girl bit her on the knee.

"Sheer folly, if you ask me."

Seg ignored Roc's provocation—it was only an ironic gauze covering a beautiful weld. "I also thought about naming her after Eck," she said, "but that felt wrong too. This one wasn't raised by snakes, she was raised by severed limbs."

"That's the most morbid thing I've ever heard," Roc said.

"But it's the truth."

"And is that what you're going to tell her when she grows up and starts asking all those damn questions? The truth?"

"I'll tell her a similar truth, the one that really matters," Seg replied.

"Which is?"

"That she evaporated here."

"Ha!" Roc exclaimed. "I suppose Zag had to pass her non-sense on to someone, and it might as well be you. But come on, girl, out with it—they're already serving dinner up there and I won't stand to eat cold food. Just tell me her damn name so we can move on already."

"I haven't named her yet," Seg said. "I realized, after all this time, that I like *my* name. And then I vaguely recalled that you were the one who gave it to me. So, what do you say, Roc? Can you think of another?"

"Cheryl," Roc said, and turned to walk up the Incline.

"Come on, Roc. Seriously." Seg grabbed the girl by the hand and pulled her along, trying to catch up to the old Plumbess. "Three letters, one syllable—she's going to be a Plumbess."

"We'll see what Plumbess Tes has to say about that."

"Plumbess Tes? *How is she still alive?*"

Made in the USA
Middletown, DE
12 July 2022

68996787R00144